TWISTED REVENGE

M A COMLEY

JEAMEL PUBLISHING LIMITED

New York Times and USA Today bestselling author M A Comley
Published by Jeamel Publishing limited
Copyright © 2020 M A Comley
Digital Edition, License Notes

ALSO BY M A COMLEY

Blind Justice (Novella)

Cruel Justice (Book #1)

Mortal Justice (Novella)

Impeding Justice (Book #2)

Final Justice (Book #3)

Foul Justice (Book #4)

Guaranteed Justice (Book #5)

Ultimate Justice (Book #6)

Virtual Justice (Book #7)

Hostile Justice (Book #8)

Tortured Justice (Book #9)

Rough Justice (Book #10)

Dubious Justice (Book #11)

Calculated Justice (Book #12)

Twisted Justice (Book #13)

Justice at Christmas (Short Story)

Justice at Christmas 2 (novella)

Prime Justice (Book #14)

Heroic Justice (Book #15)

Shameful Justice (Book #16)

Immoral Justice (Book #17)

Toxic Justice (Book #18)

Overdue Justice (Book #19)

Unfair Justice (a 10,000 word short story)

Irrational Justice (a 10,000 word short story)

Seeking Justice (a 15,000 word novella)

Caring For Justice (a 24,000 word novella)

Savage Justice (a 17,000 word novella Featuring THE UNICORN)

Clever Deception (co-written by Linda S Prather)

Tragic Deception (co-written by Linda S Prather)

Sinful Deception (co-written by Linda S Prather)

Forever Watching You (DI Miranda Carr thriller)

Wrong Place (DI Sally Parker thriller #1)

No Hiding Place (DI Sally Parker thriller #2)

Cold Case (DI Sally Parker thriller#3)

Deadly Encounter (DI Sally Parker thriller #4)

Lost Innocence (DI Sally Parker thriller #5)

Goodbye, My Precious Child (DI Sally Parker #6)

Web of Deceit (DI Sally Parker Novella with Tara Lyons)

The Missing Children (DI Kayli Bright #1)

Killer On The Run (DI Kayli Bright #2)

Hidden Agenda (DI Kayli Bright #3)

Murderous Betrayal (Kayli Bright #4)

Dying Breath (Kayli Bright #5)

Taken (Kayli Bright #6 coming March 2020)

The Hostage Takers (DI Kayli Bright Novella)

No Right to Kill (DI Sara Ramsey #1)

Killer Blow (DI Sara Ramsey #2)

The Dead Can't Speak (DI Sara Ramsey #3)

Deluded (DI Sara Ramsey #4)

The Murder Pact (DI Sara Ramsey #5)

Twisted Revenge (DI Sara Ramsey #6)

The Caller (co-written with Tara Lyons)

Evil In Disguise – a novel based on True events

Deadly Act (Hero series novella)

Torn Apart (Hero series #1)

End Result (Hero series #2)

In Plain Sight (Hero Series #3)

Double Jeopardy (Hero Series #4)

Criminal Actions (Hero Series #5)

Sole Intention (Intention series #1)

Grave Intention (Intention series #2)

Devious Intention (Intention #3)

Merry Widow (A Lorne Simpkins short story)

It's A Dog's Life (A Lorne Simpkins short story)

A Time To Heal (A Sweet Romance)

A Time For Change (A Sweet Romance)

High Spirits

The Temptation series (Romantic Suspense/New Adult Novellas)

Past Temptation

Lost Temptation

Cozy Mystery Series

Murder at the Wedding

Murder at the Hotel

Murder by the Sea

Tempting Christa (A billionaire romantic suspense co-authored by Tracie Delaney #1)

Avenging Christa (A billionaire romantic suspense co-authored by Tracie Delaney #2)

ACKNOWLEDGMENTS

Thank you as always to my rock, Jean, I'd be lost without you in my life.

Special thanks as always go to @studioenp for their superb cover design expertise.

My heartfelt thanks go to my wonderful editor Emmy Ellis, my proofreaders Joseph, Barbara and Jacqueline for spotting all the lingering nits.

Thank you to Gail for allowing me to create a character in your honour.

To Mary, gone, but never forgotten. I hope you found the peace you were searching for my dear friend.

PROLOGUE

*A*listair Daly was a workaholic. He'd built his business up from absolutely nothing. Granted, it had taken him eighteen years, but the trials and tribulations had all been worth it. Of course, his wife, Gail, had a lot to do with that success, so why had he treated her so poorly in the past? He was guilty of being a man with yearnings that ultimately needed satisfying. Over the years, he'd had the opportunity to embark on various flings, none of them lasting that long, and yet Gail had always stuck by him.

His latest fling had lasted around six weeks. She had exhausted him, what with her being twenty years his junior. She'd stroked his ego, and so much more during their time together. Sadly, the girl had fallen for him, and he'd had to call an end to their brief affair.

That was all in the past. Now he had a bright new future ahead of him. Exciting plans for expansion had just been passed by the bank and the council, and he was on his way home to his beautiful wife, to celebrate their twentieth anniversary. From now on, he would be devoting all his energy to their marriage. Intent on mending his ways, he made a vow never to look at another woman. *I wonder how long that's going to last.*

He'd ensure it did—this time. During his numerous affairs, he'd never once thought about deserting Gail. He'd always loved her. All he'd ever needed was to service his needs.

He smiled as his wife's beautiful features filled his mind. He had a lot of making up to do tonight. He went into the office and retrieved a couple of items from the safe. The first was the overnight banking bag, which he intended dropping off on his way home, and the second was an exquisite eternity ring he'd had specially commissioned for Gail. She wasn't expecting it. He'd regrettably let her down in that department, too, only acknowledging their anniversaries a few times in two decades.

His cheeks heated. He was embarrassed to admit how badly he'd treated Gail. *A new beginning. All that is about to change now. She and the kids deserve so much more than I've ever given them.*

He locked the safe and the office and strode across the yard to ensure all the outbuildings were secured for the evening, then he walked through the main gate. Padlock in hand, he tucked the night safe bag between his legs while he attached the lock.

A thump to the back of the head caused him to fall against the gates. Startled, he turned to face two people in masks.

"Open the gate," the taller one said, his voice muffled by the clown mask.

Alistair did as he was instructed. Once the gate was unlocked, the intruders bundled him inside and shut it after them.

"What is this? Please, don't hurt me. Here are the takings, I won't object. Just take them and go."

The intruders both laughed and took it in turns shoving him across the yard, heading for the office.

"Keys?" The smaller one held out a gloved hand.

Alistair dropped the office keys into the open palm and shook his head. "Please, my family are expecting me. I don't want to be late."

"Tough. Get in there." He was roughly pushed into the office.

"Please. You've got what you need. There's nearly ten thousand in the bag. Let me go, I'm begging you."

Tall leaned forward, touching his mask against Alistair's face. "Don't tell me what to do. In other words, keep frigging quiet, you're already doing my head in. We're going to have some fun with you tonight, whether you're up for it or not."

"What? Why? Please...won't you reconsider?" Alistair begged.

The man nutted him. Blood trickled into Alistair's eye from the wound. His head became fuzzy from the blow. He stumbled a little. The intruders laughed and pushed him between them, then they spun him around, adding to his confusion. Bile rose in his throat. Determined to hang on to the contents of his stomach, he swallowed the acid, or at least, he tried to.

"Please," he pitifully pleaded again.

"Please what? You want some more? Oh, don't worry, we've only just begun. We have plenty more planned for you, buster."

"Why? Why are you doing this? Do I know you? Have we met? I don't remember doing the dirty on anyone lately. Who are you?"

"Shut up!" Tall shouted in his face.

Alistair turned away from him. Even though they were both wearing masks, he didn't have to be a genius to figure out how angry they were and that they had an agenda, which included working him over a little, judging by what had gone on so far. He decided to keep schtum, for now.

"Where's the safe?" Tall asked his mate.

"In the corner, over there."

Alistair peered into the person's eyes. "How do you know that? You've been in this office? You must have been..."

Before he could finish, Tall punched him in the stomach. He doubled over, the impact taking his breath away.

He was at a loss what to do next, puzzled by their willingness to keep hurting him, despite already having the cash at their disposal.

"You know the code?" Tall asked his accomplice.

"Only he does."

Alistair was forced upright and thrust towards the back of the office where the safe was situated. Tall kicked the back of his knees. He sank down to the floor, his legs jarring.

"There's nothing inside. It's all in the bag, I swear."

"Then you won't mind opening it and proving that to us."

His hand shaking, Alistair punched in the number. The safe clicked. He eased it open, dreading what would happen to him next when they realised he was lying. There was at least another ten grand inside.

The taller one bent to view the interior. His head slowly twisted to face Alistair. He gulped, fearing what the man was going to do next.

"Once a liar, eh? Naughty boy. You were given the opportunity and you screwed it up. Get up."

"I'm sorry. Please forgive me." He scrambled to his feet, his legs complaining about the sudden movement and almost collapsing beneath him.

The pair emptied the safe, placing the money in another night bag which Alistair kept at the side of the safe.

"I think we're done here. Let's go," the smaller of the two suggested.

"What? Are you kidding me? No way. We're going to have some more fun with this arsehole. Don't be such a coward. Now, stand aside and leave him to me."

Alistair's bowels almost gave way on him.

Tall got close and dipped his head so it was level with Alistair's. "What else have you got lying around here that is worth nicking?"

"Nothing, except stock."

"And what do you think I'm likely to do with that?"

"I don't know. All I did was answer your question."

"You have a smart mouth. You're going to regret that, mate." He laughed and shoved Alistair out of the office and into the yard. "Show me where the tools are."

"In there. It's all locked up."

"Doh! Well, fix that. Unlock it, you dick."

"You have the keys," he uttered quietly.

Shorty stepped forward and unlocked the storeroom. The three of them entered. They shoved Alistair ahead and rummaged through the shelves. Tall paused and eyed the nail guns. Alistair gulped. They weren't cheap, all worth a pretty penny.

"There are some top-of-the-range drills over there." He pointed to the back at the head-high shelving unit.

4

"I like the look of this. Set it up for me. I've always wanted to have a go at one of these."

"It needs charging first," Alistair blustered.

"He's lying," Shorty was quick to add.

Alistair closed his eyes and waited for the punches to rain down on him again. Footsteps approached. A jab to the stomach, and once his head had dipped his hair was pulled back.

"Don't mess with me, shithead. Or things could turn nasty, quickly."

"I'm sorry. I didn't mean to…"

"Shut the fuck up. How does it work?"

"There's a socket over there, behind the counter. Plug it in, and I'll give you a demonstration."

"No funny business," he warned, twisting Alistair's arm behind his back.

He winced through the pain. "You have my word on that."

Alistair withdrew one of the better-quality nail guns from the shelf and took it over to the counter to assemble. He inserted the nails in the cavity and plugged it in. He kept a sample of wood behind the counter, and he fired a few nails into it. The noise was deafening in the confines of the storeroom. *I could use it on them, couldn't I?*

He didn't get the chance as Tall snatched it away from him. "I love it. Get out of my way. I want to have a play."

Alistair stood aside, eyeing the intruder and his movements, getting ready to jump out of the way if he turned and aimed the gun at him.

Instead, the guy pummelled the piece of wood with nail after nail until the chamber was empty. He glanced at Alistair. "Well, don't just stand there, fill it up, I'm enjoying this."

Alistair sprang forward and filled the gun, then stepped back again.

Tall laughed continuously as he moved on to a second piece of scrap wood he found lying behind the counter. "Right, I think I've got the hang of this now. Wait here, I've got an idea." He left the storeroom and returned a few seconds later carrying a front door from the yard.

Puzzled, Alistair watched him place it up against the shelving. "Okay, stand there," Tall ordered.

Alistair shook his head. "I won't do it."

The guy was quick. He lunged at Alistair and punched him in the face. "You'll do as I say, or else…"

The pair dragged Alistair into position up against the door.

"Please, don't do this. I have a wife and kids to consider."

They laughed at him.

"It's a pity you haven't considered them in the past," Shorty said.

Alistair tilted his head. "Do I know you?" he asked again.

"Enough chit-chat. Shut the fuck up and take your punishment like a man."

"You don't have to do this. I can get you more money, if that's what you're after."

"It's not, but thanks for the offer."

The smaller one kicked Alistair's legs apart, and the man holding the nail gun went to work. He nailed Alistair into a star shape against the door through his clothes. Alistair kept his eyes closed throughout, shitting himself to think what might happen if the man's hand slipped.

Once he was fully pinned into position, the two of them stood back to admire their work and high-fived each other.

"Okay, that'll do for preparation. Now let the games begin. I need to grab a few more tools first. Watch him. If he tries to break free, hit him in the nuts with this." Tall held up a short piece of four-by-four and left the area.

"Please, who are you? Why are you doing this to me? What have I ever done to you?" His bowels shifted through the fear.

"Plenty. You're scum. You come across as a genuine character, but nothing could be further from the truth. You use people all the time. You used *me*."

"What? So I do know you. Who are you? Please, let me try to put right the wrongs I've committed. This has gone far enough now, you've had your fun, let me go. I promise not to say anything to anyone. I'll never go to the police, I swear."

Shorty stepped into his personal space. "You won't get the chance to tell anyone. People like you deserve all that's coming to you. It's called karma, and she can be an absolute bitch at times."

"Karma...as far as I know, I've never done anything wrong. I'm fair to my employees. You do work for me, don't you? You must do, otherwise you wouldn't have known where the safe was."

"You'll never know. It'll be our secret. Yet another little secret like the others we've shared in the past."

"What? I don't have a clue what that's supposed to..."

"You two getting reacquainted again, are you? Well, enough of that. This is where the fun really begins."

He placed a few tools and a number of differently sized nails on the counter. After seeing those, Alistair could no longer hang on, and his bowels gave way on him.

"Jesus, the bastard just shat himself," Tall said. "Not the big 'I am' after all, eh, man?"

"I've never professed to be anything other than a decent human being. Please, won't you reconsider? You've had your fun. Let me go. My family...won't you think about them?"

The man growled and got in his face. "Like you did? When you screwed around behind their backs, and you have the audacity to call yourself a decent human being? In your dreams, man. You're nothing but a lowdown, worthless piece of shit." He rubbed his gloved hands together. "Let the good times roll. Do you want to go first?"

Shorty's head shook. "Nope, he's all yours. I'll take more pleasure from watching him suffer. I want to witness the pain in his eyes as you torture him."

"Please, there's no need for any of this. You have the money," Alistair pleaded, his voice croaky with emotion as tears bulged, threatening to fall.

"Oh, but there is. Just lie back and enjoy it. How many times have you said that to the women you've screwed over the years, eh?"

"Never. I swear. You've got this all wrong. I love my wife and..."

The shorter one struck him across the face. "Liar. You *fucking* liar. You never loved her, you couldn't have."

"All right. Let's get this show on the road," the taller one said, getting between Alistair and his accomplice. He pushed his associate back a little and reached for one of the hammers and a four-inch nail.

"No, don't do this…" Alistair said, tears running down his cheeks.

Shorty came closer and spread Alistair's right hand apart. The other one pressed the nail into Alistair's palm and bashed it in with the hammer. He screamed out, the pain unbearable. The other two stood there and chuckled.

The shorter one drifted out of his peripheral vision and returned carrying a piece of oily rag which was shoved in Alistair's mouth, preventing him from alerting the neighbours or anyone else who might be walking past.

"This is fun. Next one."

Shorty forced open Alistair's other hand, and again Tall hammered in a nail. A muffled cry from Alistair did nothing to stop the smaller one from ripping the buttons off Alistair's shirt, exposing his hairy chest. His breathing had become erratic, according to the rise and fall on show. He shook his head from side to side, an inaudible plea being ignored by his attackers.

"Are you sure you don't want a go? It's such a thrill," Tall asked.

"No. It gives me more pleasure to see him squirm. Do it!"

Another nail sank into his flesh, this time scraping past one of his ribs. The pain was enough to make Alistair want to vomit, however, if he did that, he'd almost certainly die of suffocation. Maybe that would be a preferable option to what these two had planned for him. He closed his eyes, trying to block out their actions. They suddenly sprang open again when another nail pierced his flesh, this time in the top of his leg. *Shit! What have I done to deserve this? Make them stop, please. Someone please come and help me.* He knew there was little hope of anyone doing that. Granted, Gail might ring the office or his mobile if he didn't return home within the next half an hour. There again, she might give up on him—after all, he'd let her down dozens of times in the past, either stopping off at the pub on the way home or visiting one of his lady friends, rather than spend time with her.

Jesus, what a bastard I've been over the years. Is this truly the way my life is going to end?

Another nail, this time to his other leg, just above the knee. All at strategic points throughout his body, avoiding any main arteries or organs. Was it their intention to draw out the torture? It had to be. He opened his eyes a touch, his gaze blurry from yet more unshed tears. "Please, don't do this."

His voice, stifled, went unnoticed as the couple decided where the next strike should be.

He squeezed his eyes shut once more and winced when another nail hit its target, on his left side between the ribs again. The next one pierced his upper right arm. The one after that, his left. His right leg was targeted again next. By now, he was weak from the pain and loss of blood. *Let me go now before things turn more sinister.*

Another nail was fired into his stomach. *Please, let me die! I can't bear it any longer.*

One more, this time to the edge of his neck. More giggling from his attackers. At least they were having fun. He wasn't.

Tall removed the cloth from his mouth. "Anything you want to say?"

"No," he whispered weakly.

"That's a shame. Okay, farewell, big man. It's been a pleasure. Your type don't deserve happiness. Causing people pain has been your main ambition in this life. Karma strikes again…"

His eyes closed as the nail came towards his head. The point lingered on his forehead, and then…

1

"What are your plans for this evening?" Mark stood behind her and placed his arms around her waist while she applied the lightest of makeup ready for work.

Sara smiled. "Why? What do you have planned?"

"A night in, you, me and the cat. I'll cook us a nice meal, and we can discuss wedding plans, how does that sound?"

"Great. Oh gosh, hold that thought, my phone is vibrating."

He dropped his arms and slipped into the bathroom, giving her the privacy she needed to take the call. He was good like that, considerate and aware she had a busy work life. So did he, and that was why they made the perfect couple.

"Hello. DI Ramsey. How can I help?"

Misty the cat sat on the bed, demanding her usual attention. Sara stroked her back and pulled her tail a little at the end. Her purring grew loud, proving how much she enjoyed the feel of Sara's touch.

"Morning, ma'am, it's Jeff Makepeace. Sorry to disturb you so early, thought you'd want to hear about this one right away."

"This one? A new case? What is it, Jeff?"

"A gruesome one. My lads reported back to me saying they'd never seen anything like it in all their years on the force."

"That bodes well." She hadn't meant to let the sarcasm slip out. "Where?"

"On the edge of Hereford at the Brinkwell Trading Estate."

"I know it. What part?"

"There's a builders' merchants down there called Daly's. The owner is the one who has carked it."

"Carked it? Is that a local term, Jeff?" She sniggered, still trying to come to terms with the local dialect after moving down from Manchester around three years earlier, when her husband was brutally murdered by a ruthless gang. The same gang who had kidnapped Mark, not long after they had started seeing each other.

"Sorry, ma'am. The owner is the victim at the scene."

"That's better terminology, I much prefer that. Okay, I'm just about to leave here anyway. I'll go directly to the scene. With the heavy traffic at this time of the morning, I probably won't be there for another twenty-five to thirty minutes. Have you contacted DS Jameson yet?"

"I'm about to do that now. Shall I request she meets you there?"

"Do that, thanks, Jeff."

Mark came back into the room as she tucked the phone in her jacket pocket. "I've got to fly. Another murder in town. Hold that thought about the wedding plans. I have no idea how long my day is going to turn out to be, you know how it is, hon."

He kissed her, a kiss that took her breath away.

"I do. Don't worry, it'll keep until the weekend if it has to. Ring me during the day if you get the chance."

"Of course I will. Sorry to let you down."

"Nonsense, you've done no such thing. Stay safe out there."

She smiled and touched his cheek. "You have enough to worry about being a vet, don't go getting distracted thinking about me. I wouldn't want you to give the wrong dog the snip."

He laughed. "Christ, can you imagine the uproar that would bring? I promise to keep my mind on the job at all times."

Sara stroked Misty again and rushed down the stairs and into the kitchen. She quickly fed her precious companion and promised Mark she'd empty Misty's cat tray when she arrived home that evening.

He shooed her out the front door. "No need, I'll do it now. I have a spare couple of minutes before I'll need to set off."

"You're a treasure. Thank you. Have a good day." Another swift kiss, and she flew out of the door and into her car.

"In a rush as usual, I see, Sara."

She spun around, a smile already in place, recognising her neighbour's voice. "Morning, Ted, how's things?"

"You haven't got time to hear my woes. Have a good one."

"I'll be around later, hopefully. Drop by and have a chat if you need me."

He waved away her concerns. "Get on with you, we're fine. Speak soon."

"Say hi to Mavis for me. We'll arrange to have dinner shortly."

"That would be super. It's our turn to entertain, if I remember rightly."

"It is." She closed the car door and turned the key. Her faithful car sprang into life, even on the chilliest of mornings.

Driving into Hereford, there was a haze of fog in front of her. She shuddered. Was this a sign of what to expect at the scene? She switched on the CD player and slotted in an old favourite of hers, a Motown compilation that had her tapping her fingers on the steering wheel in no time at all. As expected, the traffic was horrendous as she approached Roman Road. With all the new-build estates going up, she only envisaged things getting worse instead of better in the months and years ahead. Diana Ross filled the car and lessened her aggravation a touch.

Her nerves were in tatters by the time she pulled into the trading estate. She spotted Carla's car and the pathologist's van parked side by side in the far corner. After donning a paper suit, she held up her ID to the officious uniformed officer blocking her way.

"Sorry, ma'am."

"No need to apologise. Glad to see you're doing your job properly, Constable."

"Thank you, ma'am. I hope you haven't eaten a large breakfast. It ain't pretty."

"I haven't. Thanks for the warning," she replied, grateful she hadn't had time to consume anything before leaving home. She entered the yard and called out, "Hello, where are you both?"

"In here. The storeroom on the right," Carla's voice filtered back to her.

She shivered. The yard was giving off a cold, eerie atmosphere. She stepped into the storeroom and paused in the doorway. "Bloody Nora! Oh God, good job my stomach is empty. What the heck is wrong with people?"

Lorraine, the nutty pathologist, and one of her best friends, enticed her to come closer. "Don't be shy."

"Do I have to? Can't you give me your assessment without me coming nearer?"

"Nope, it doesn't work like that and you know it. He's dead, he isn't about to rise up like Jesus—at least I hope not. Someone saw fit to crucify the poor man."

"No shit, Sherlock. That much I can bloody see for myself. What possesses a sane person to want to do that to another human being? Jesus, what a frigging warped world we live in."

Carla and Lorraine shook hands, and Lorraine passed a fiver to Carla. Sara frowned.

Carla winked at Sara. "We had a bet on what you'd say when you saw the victim."

Sara's eyes bulged. "You what? Are you telling me I'm bloody predictable?" she demanded, incensed by their behaviour. *What a great way to start a day!*

"Oops, didn't mean to cause offence. Don't blame Carla, it was all my idea," Lorraine said.

"Why am I not surprised about that? Sodding hell, you get worse as you age, not better."

Lorraine grinned. "I'll take that as a compliment."

"Take it however you frigging like. Right, give me the lowdown on what you have so far—no going around the houses or making stupid wisecracks either. Let's treat the damn victim with a bit of respect for a change, shall we?"

"A tad harsh. One slip-up and you blow things out of all proportion."

"Whatever. Get on with it and stop trying my bloody patience."

"Someone either got out of the bed the wrong side this morning or failed to get laid last night," Lorraine grumbled.

Sara threw her hands up in the air. They fell back down and slapped against her thighs. "I give up. Carla, perhaps you'll do me the courtesy of filling me in?"

"I'd rather Lorraine did it, boss," her partner replied sheepishly.

"You're both as bad as one another and need a kick up the jacksy. I'll willingly oblige later if I hear one more ounce of tripe coming out of either of your mouths. Now, professional heads on, ladies, and tell me what we have here."

Carla and Lorraine both had the decency to appear to be sorry for their childish behaviour. Therefore, she was willing to accept their awkwardness and move on.

"To my reckoning, the poor man was still alive when the torture began. The murderer was careful while inserting the nails, avoiding all the main arteries and organs, to prolong the man's agony."

"Is that a rag in his mouth?" Sara asked, taking a step closer to the victim.

"It is. I'll need to examine it to see if it was soaked in petrol or if it's just an oily rag the assailant found lying around and decided to use," Lorraine informed her.

Sara sniffed the air. "I can't smell any petrol, can you?" She made an invisible strike in the air. *Stick that where the sun don't shine, lady pathologist.*

"Okay, you got me on that one," Lorraine admitted.

Sara smirked, enjoying her friend's sudden discomfort. "Go on, I'm only teasing, or was I getting my own back? What else can you tell me?"

"Nothing much except the victim was in an excruciating amount of pain throughout."

"I figured that much out for myself, thanks, Lorraine. I take it the nail in his forehead was the one that killed him, right?"

"Nothing wrong with your powers of deduction, Madam Detective. The poor man must have suffered for a long time before that final blow took his last breath."

"Disgusting, I agree." Sara glanced over her shoulder into the yard. "Who found him?"

Carla tutted and sucked in a breath. "His bloody sister. She works here and opened up this morning."

"Shit! Stupid question, but is she all right?"

Lorraine pointed to a patch of vomit a few feet away. "She lost her stomach the second she laid eyes on him. Only natural, I suppose."

Sara nodded, thinking she would have likely done the same if she'd discovered a member of her own family in such a state. It didn't alter the fact the scene had likely been contaminated. "Where is she now?"

"In the office. I made her a strong cup of sweet tea as soon as I arrived," Carla said.

"Anyone with her?"

"Yes, a female officer."

Sara sighed. "We'll need to question her. Has she said anything, apart from the obvious?"

"She told me she'd rung her brother's wife to tell her. Saved us a job," Carla added.

"Hmm…not the way I would have preferred things to happen, but what's done is done. I need to have a chat with her. Anything you want to add, Lorraine?"

"No. Only that you should be on the lookout for a sadistic individual who gets his or her kicks out of hurting their victims."

"Him or her? Are you saying a woman could be guilty of doing this?"

Lorraine shrugged. "Given the equipment used and the way he was attached to the door, yes, it's possible a woman could have done this. Maybe she had some form of hold over him, you know, which might have prevented him from putting up a struggle to begin with."

Sara's brow furrowed. "Not sure how you've come to that conclusion, but I'll bear it in mind during the investigation."

"Pure speculation on my part. Any normal person would have put up some sort of fight in the circumstances, true?"

"If you say so. Okay, I'm going to see what the sister can tell me. We'll leave you to it, Lorraine."

Carla followed Sara out into the yard and tugged on her arm. "I want to apologise for my behaviour back there. I'm hoping you won't hold it against me."

Sara punched her partner gently in the top of the arm. "You're forgiven, this time. If it happens again, it'll be a different story."

Carla mock-saluted. "Sorry, it won't, I promise."

Sara nodded. "The trouble is, I'm aware of what a bad influence Lorraine can be."

"You're not wrong. You should've heard the wisecracks she was firing off in there until you showed up."

"Disrespectful mare. I swear she's getting worse. Don't go down the same route, Carla, I like you just the way you are. Start copying her and her values, and you and I are going to fall out, got that?"

"Loud and clear. I'm sorry."

She smiled. "Enough with the apologies, let's push on. We have a killer out there, and I intend arresting them before the end of the month. Our targets have been shite so far. Let's see if we can rectify that by solving this case in record time."

"Wow, you're expecting us to do that within two days?"

Sara chewed on her bottom lip. "Two days might be stretching it a little. Let's think positive about it, though."

"I hate it when our policing skills are called into question because of the targets we have to maintain."

"That makes two of us. No point in us worrying about it. Where's the sister? Did you get her name?"

"It's Emma. The office is over here." Carla pointed off to the left.

"Let's get cracking then. Strong resolve—I think this is going to be a tough one, just saying."

Carla tutted. "I fear you might be right."

Together, they entered the office. Emma sat behind a huge oak desk, her head buried in her hands. Sara dismissed the officer standing guard inside the door and approached the desk, her warrant card on show in case Emma looked up.

"Emma, I'm DI Sara Ramsey, the Senior Investigating Officer. I'm so sorry for your loss. Are you up to answering some questions? I quite understand if you're not."

Emma wiped the sleeve of her jumper across her eyes. "If I have to. I want this person caught, so I'm willing to do just about anything."

Sara and Carla sat in chairs opposite her. Carla had her pen and notebook poised ready to jot down any likely answers.

Sara exhaled a large breath. "In your own time, can you tell me what happened when you arrived at work this morning? In as much detail as you're comfortable with."

"My brother is usually here before me, so I didn't take any notice of the gates being open when I got here. I parked next to his car as usual."

"So were the gates wide open or pulled to but unlocked?"

"Pulled to, just the way we leave them when only one of us is here. We tend to open them fully once everyone has arrived and we're open for business, does that make sense?"

"It does. You're doing fine. What happened next?" Sara asked, prompting Emma with a brief smile of encouragement.

"I began searching for Alistair. It was his wedding anniversary yesterday. I was eager to know how the evening went with Gail, that's his wife. I came in here—he's usually in the office first thing dealing with the post and any overnight calls on the answerphone. The office was empty." She wiped a stray tear from her cheek, then continued, "It wasn't until I left the office that I noticed the storeroom door was ajar. We've got stocktaking in a few weeks; I thought he might be in there checking the stock, you know, to see what needed to be ordered before the big day arrived. That's when I found him..."

"It's okay, take your time. Was he dead when you found him?" Sara cringed, thinking the question sounded callous even to her own ears. She kicked herself for not asking Lorraine what she thought the time of death was. *Damn that woman for ticking me off, swiping me off my usual stride.*

"Yes. After I vomited, I plucked up the courage to approach him. I ran my hand down his face—he was cold to the touch. I rested my head on his chest for a moment. I'm sorry, I couldn't help myself. We were very close, you see."

"It's okay, there's no need for you to be concerned about that. It's a natural thing to do when someone discovers a loved one in those circumstances. What did you do next?"

"I rang the police. I was too distraught to ring Gail at that point. Then it dawned on me that the murderer might still be around. I ran in here and locked myself in until your colleagues arrived."

"I see. That was a good move. Well done, you can't be too careful these days. Is that when you contacted his wife?"

"Yes. I should be there with her. Don't tell me I did the wrong thing calling her? I'd hate that."

"No, I wouldn't tell you that at all. Gail has a right to know, and you would be the best person to tell her."

"Then why do I feel like shit about ringing her? I think I did it arse about face. I should have driven over there. It's not the type of thing someone should hear over the phone, is it? No, I realise that now. She's going to be so narked at me once the reality hits."

"There's no right or wrong way to share the news that a loved one has departed. I'm sure she'll be fine. Once things have settled, she'll appreciate hearing the news from you rather than us."

"But she shouldn't be alone. I should be with her."

"Does she have children?"

"Yes, a boy of fourteen and a girl of sixteen."

"Would they have still been at home when you rang her?"

"Yes, she was in the middle of fixing their breakfast."

"I see. Then your sister-in-law won't be alone."

"I guess. There will be three distraught people in the house instead of only one. I need to get over there to make sure everyone is okay."

"We can arrange to get you there soon, I promise. How long have you worked with your brother?"

"Around eighteen years, since this place opened."

"How many employees do you have?"

"There are ten here."

"Has Alistair had any problems with his staff recently?"

Emma shook her head. "No, not as far as I know." She covered her face with her shaking hands as if it had just dawned on her all over again what she'd lost.

"It's okay. You're allowed to cry. We won't judge you, Emma," Sara said softly.

With that, the sobs came and the tears flowed.

Sara glanced Carla's way. "Can you source us some coffee?"

Her partner pushed back her chair and left Sara to deal with the grieving Emma.

"Are you all right, Emma?"

Emma dropped her hands, and she stared at Sara through red, sore eyes. "I don't think I'll ever be the same again after seeing him like that. Oh shit! Our parents...they're elderly. How the hell am I going to break the news to them?"

"I can help, if that's what you want, although experience tells me that this type of news is always better coming from another family member."

Fresh tears gathered and slowly escaped her eyes. "No, they will want to hear it from me. Who? For what reason?"

"That was going to be my next question. Do you keep any money on site? Or do builders generally buy through an account?"

"A bit of both really." She swivelled her chair and darted to the back of the office where she crouched.

"Wait...don't touch anything!" Sara strained her neck to see what she was up to. All became apparent once a clunk sounded. *A safe!*

"No, the money has gone, and yet the safe was secured again."

"Okay, that will give us a motive. We could be looking at a burglary. Is it common knowledge that money is kept on site?"

"I don't think so. It's not, not really. Alistair goes to the night safe on his way home every evening." She held up a cloth bag, emphasising her point, and then returned and flopped into her seat.

"He had a routine then. Did he leave at the same time every night?"

"Thereabouts, unless we've had a late delivery. He was anal about putting the stock away in its rightful place. I've never met such a tidy bloke. Oh God…has he really gone? I can't believe it. We're all going to miss him so much. The kids are going to be lost without him; they were all very close. He used to take them to various clubs at the weekend. Who will do that for them now?"

"Gail will have to step in, won't she?" Sara suggested.

"I suppose I can help out occasionally. So, you think this is a burglary? Do burglars tend to torture people? I thought I heard on TV that most burglaries lacked any form of violence and took place when the house was empty. Am I wrong about that?"

"No, statistics back that idea up, but honestly, there are always exceptions to the rule. Maybe we're looking at an organised gang here, or at least more than one person. I don't know. Everything is up in the air until SOCO and the pathologist can give us some leads to follow."

Carla entered the room carrying three paper cups on a plank of scrap wood. "It was all I could find." She shrugged and placed the cups in front of them all.

Emma picked up her cup and cradled it in her hands. She stared at the desk, appearing to be mesmerised by a certain spot.

Sara had an inkling about the turmoil she was going through. Losing Philip the way she had had devastated her at the time. She'd shut everyone out for weeks, even her own family. Until her parents had eventually sat her down and explained that life must go on and not to shut her loved ones out. It had been the wake-up call she'd needed to get on with her life. Misty had helped her pull through the darkest of days until Mark had drifted into her life. All the pain and misery were long behind her now…she hoped.

Carla nudged Sara's knee with her own, jolting her out of her reverie. Sara rolled her eyes and mouthed an apology.

"Are the staff all here?" Sara asked.

Emma glanced up and nodded. "Most of them. Two are missing, though; they're on holiday."

"Where?"

"One in the Caribbean and the other in America. Are you saying you think a member of our staff did this?"

"It's an option we have to consider. If not them, then it's possible an acquaintance of theirs could be responsible. I know this is a really upsetting time for you, but if you could give us all their names and addresses, our enquiries will be a whole lot smoother."

"Of course. Oh my, you've floored me. You seriously think someone who knew him could treat him like that?"

"I know it's hard to believe. It's surprising what motives we've come across over the years, I can tell you. Either someone who works here or possibly a customer could have done this. But if you're telling me that Alistair hasn't fallen out with anyone lately, then the likelihood that this could be a one-off and it's a criminal chancing their arm can't be ruled out either."

"Wow, okay, so many different possibilities. No wonder your job is tough." Emma offered a weak smile.

"That's so true. If only criminals committed the crimes and then handed themselves in, it would make our jobs so much easier. Unfortunately, it doesn't work like that in the real world."

"I get it. I'll drink my coffee and then search through the personnel files."

"Perhaps you could give us a list of employees who have left the firm in the past year, too. Would you mind?"

"Of course. There haven't been that many, one or two. People tend to remain with us for years. That's why I find it incredible that you think an employee could have done this."

"It's better to cover all the bases right from the outset, Emma. Do you have any other siblings?"

"Yes, another brother. He's a gas fitter by trade. Always in and out of here. Shit! I haven't rung Des yet."

"Do you want to do that now?"

She reached for the phone, placed it to her ear, and then put it down again. "I can't use that, it smells of him."

Sara handed her mobile across the desk. "Use my phone instead. Do you know his number?"

"Yes, it's imprinted in my mind. I'm always handing his cards out to customers."

"I see. Do you want us to leave?"

"No, I'm fine. I think I'd rather you were here. It might help me hold it together more."

Sara nodded.

Emma tapped the number into the phone, and her gaze drifted out of the small window overlooking the yard. "Hi, Des, it's me. Where are you? Oh right, I'll see you when you get here. Come straight to the office." She handed the phone back to Sara after she ended the call. "Oh God. He's two minutes away. He'll go ballistic if he sees you lot here."

"May I ask why? Are you saying he has a temper?" Sara asked, puzzled.

"No." She dipped her head and then said, "He doesn't care much for the police. A friend of his was arrested on false charges a few years ago. He's been trying to get his sentence quashed ever since."

"Right, thanks for the warning. Is he likely to kick off when he learns of what happened to Alistair?"

She nodded and chewed on the inside of her mouth. "Yes. I hope I'm wrong about that, but be prepared for a backlash."

"Okay. Carla, perhaps you can instruct one of the uniformed officers to join us, just in case."

Carla left the room again and returned with one of the burliest officers available on site. Instead of feeling worried, Sara breathed deeply again, assured by his presence.

Moments later, a thickset man with salt-and-pepper hair barged into the office. "Emma, what the heck is going on? Why are the police here? Is that a forensics van outside? I'm confused. What's going on?"

Emma was visibly shaking. "Sit down, Des."

"I won't. Not until you tell me what all this is about."

Sara decided to jump in. "Mr Daly, I'm DI Sara Ramsey. Please, sir, try to calm down. Take a seat, and we'll explain the situation."

He ran a hand through his hair, and his face screwed up in confusion. He yanked a chair from the edge of the room and placed it close to where the others were sitting. "Go on then, enlighten me," he demanded, crossing his arms across his broad chest.

Sara inhaled and exhaled a couple of breaths. "Unfortunately, when your sister arrived at work this morning, she found your brother dead."

His head swiftly turned towards his sister. "Emma, is this true?"

"Yes." She started crying again. "He was…murdered."

Des shot out of his chair. "What the actual fuck? You can't be serious?" He paced back and forth, clearly agitated.

"Sir, please calm down. You're upsetting your sister…" Sara requested, her gaze darting between the siblings.

"Calm down? Are you right in the head? How would you be reacting if you heard such devastating news?" Des snapped back.

"Des, don't do this. Alistair wouldn't want to see you angry like this," Emma pleaded, grasping his forearm.

He shrugged his sister off. "Don't give me that bullshit. You know the ruddy police are useless. I'll get the bastard who did this. I'll deal with them the way they should be dealt with. Murdering scumbags." His rage filtered into his cheeks, turning them crimson.

"You're not helping matters, sir," Sara insisted. She glanced behind her and motioned for the officer to come closer.

"What? You're going to go all heavy on me? Arrest me for shooting my mouth off, is that it?"

Emma sobbed. "Please, Des, this is hard enough without you kicking off. What's done is done. Alistair is gone, and there's not a damn thing we can do about it. Don't make this worse than it is already."

"That's it, blame me, the way you always do. Get a grip and look around woman. How many police do you see hanging around here? *Here*, when they should be out there searching for a killer before the trail goes cold. They haven't got a bloody clue these days. Locking up innocent people and yet letting real criminals get away with things scot-free."

Sara rose from her chair, anger searing her veins. "I won't say this again, Mr Daly. I need you to sit in your damn chair and calm down. Your sister is already upset enough about what's happened today. Don't make matters worse. Have some compassion for other people's feelings." *There, I've said it, you idiot! You forced me to have a pop at you, no one else.*

"How dare you speak to me in that tone? I demand to see your immediate superior. I don't want a woman in charge of my brother's case. I need someone with determination running through them to do the right thing."

"And flinging unnecessary insults around like that isn't going to do you any favours at all. For your information, sir, my immediate superior is a woman, and I have to tell you she's even bolshier than I am. I can give you her direct number, if that's what you truly want."

He plonked into the chair. Elbows on his thighs, he buried his head in his hands. "I'm sorry," he mumbled.

Sara retook her seat. "Apology accepted. I'm sorry, too, for your loss and the impact losing a loved one is clearly already having on your life. If you can put that aside for a few moments and answer some questions, I'd appreciate it."

He swallowed noisily and dropped his hands to look her in the eye. "Okay, my outburst was unforgiveable. What do you need from us?" He searched for his sister's hand.

She clenched his tightly and offered a slight smile.

"Before you arrived, we were asking Emma some questions, trying to establish if she knew of anyone on the staff who would have likely done this. She wasn't sure we were on the right track. Maybe your brother mentioned something in the past, a run-in with one of the staff, or possibly a customer?"

"He never mentioned anything to me. Alistair was a pretty amenable chap. Had a good heart and often let people off who couldn't pay their bills at the end of the month. I pulled him up about that, told him he wasn't doing these people any favours and they had to take responsibility for their debts. The trouble with today's society is that people like to spend what they haven't got and shrug off the consequences at the end of the month. If people have the goods, they need to stump up the cash. I told him he was making a rod for his own back offering credit around here. Would he listen? Like heck. Didn't I tell him, Emma? You'll vouch for me, won't you?"

"I will. If I have to. But, Des, this isn't about if you were right and Alistair was in the wrong. He's dead. The police need to ask these questions in order for them to proceed. Can you cut all the crap and just answer the specific questions the inspector asks?"

"I'm doing my best here. Don't shout at me." He glared at his sister.

"I'm sorry," Emma muttered, her head dipping to her chest.

"There's no need for either of you to apologise when emotions are running high," Sara told them.

"Okay, what else do you need to know?" Des asked.

"You haven't really answered my last question yet."

"I don't know. Would anyone owing a debt possibly stoop to such levels as to bump him off to wipe out their debts?"

"I doubt it," Emma replied. "The debts belong to the business, not Alistair as such."

"But would someone out of their mind with worry think about that? Maybe someone showed up here and pleaded with him to reconsider coming after them for payment and took a swipe at him," Des replied, messing with the stubble on his chin.

"Ordinarily, I'd probably agree with that," Sara said. "However, your brother was tortured before he lost his life."

The confusion on Des' face was clear to see. "Tortured? Here? How?"

"Please don't ask that, Des," Emma pleaded, rubbing the tears away from her eyes.

"Why shouldn't I? I have a right to know how he died. Did you see him, in all his glory?" he demanded.

"Yes. What the heck? Why are you being such an arse about this? He's dead, and that's all you need to know. After seeing what the murderer did to him, I know I'll never have a decent night's sleep again for as long as I live."

"There you go again, always relying on your stint with the amateur dramatic group to emphasise your point."

"I do not. You're such a prick at times."

"Please, I need you both to calm down. All this anger isn't getting either of you anywhere. Can we stick to the facts? All we need is a lead or two to get this started. At present, we have nothing."

"No clues? Fingerprints, blood spatter? Nothing?" Des asked, frowning.

"No, nothing as yet. SOCO and the pathologist are doing their best to rectify that. Emma, can you start making that list for me?" Sara smiled at Emma, willing her to move away from her toxic brother before she imploded.

"I'll do it now. Get your thinking cap on, Des. Let's stop being obstructive and help the inspector and her team."

Emma moved her chair closer to the filing cabinet and withdrew a handful of files. She flipped them open and jotted down the information on an A4 sheet of paper, placed them back into the drawer and repeated the task, removing yet more files.

While his sister was doing that, Des sat in his chair, appearing to be shell-shocked. He kept folding and unfolding his arms and legs, expelling the odd large breath now and again. Sara glanced sideways at Carla who rolled her eyes.

"Do you work in the immediate area, Des?"

"Yes, I cover the whole of Hereford. Why?"

"No reason. And you use this place regularly for your supplies?" Sara asked. She felt like she was clutching at straws, just to keep the conversation going between them.

"Yes, my brother has always been good to me, offered me discounts along the way. Why wouldn't I come here?"

"No reason."

The room fell silent again, except for Emma riffling through the files at the back of the office.

"How are you doing?" Sara called over when she could no longer stand the awkward atmosphere.

"Nearly there. I've listed all the staff. I'm going through the former employees now. As I said, there aren't many, so I shouldn't be too long."

"No rush, take your time." Sara flipped through her phone to see if there were any urgent messages. There weren't.

Finally, Emma wheeled her chair back to the desk and placed the sheet of paper in front of her. "These are all the employees, including the two on holiday, and those are the two former members of staff. I have no way of knowing if their addresses are current or not. The ones who have left, I mean. All the current staff inform us of any changes; we insist on our records being kept up to date at all times."

"That's helpful. Thanks for being so efficient, Emma. Would it be okay if we set up an interview room somewhere, to question the staff? I appreciate the process will take time and I wouldn't want to disrupt you by using this office."

"No, use this one. It's not as if I'm going to be able to function properly today anyway. Actually, will you need me? I'd like to visit my parents and Gail at the earliest convenience."

"I don't have a problem with that. We'll need to close the doors to the public today, if that's okay with you?"

"Of course. The place is yours. I should only be a couple of hours, I hope. Des, you can come with me."

"Shit! Do I have to? You're so much better at dealing with things like this."

"Yes, you have to. Why should I do this on my own? That wouldn't be fair, would it? Anyway, I'm in no fit state to drive."

"You're presuming I am."

"Yes. Men react better to this kind of stuff."

He groaned and left his chair. "Whatever, come on. I haven't got all day."

The siblings left the office.

Sara stared down at the list of employees. "Ten of them. Shall we divide the list in half? Would you feel comfortable questioning the staff alone?"

Carla shrugged. "You know me, I'd prefer it if you did the questioning, but as there are so many, it makes sense to divvy it up."

"That's true. Now, all we need to do is find another room we can use."

"I'll do that. You can have the office."

Sara grinned. "I was hoping you might say that." She tore the A4 sheet in half and handed Carla the top, leaving her with the names of five current employees and the two former ones. "Let's get this over with. Try and make it brief and to the point with each of them, however, ensure you don't come across as an uncaring bitch."

"Really? You felt it was necessary to prep me on how to behave with people in shock?"

"No, don't start, Carla. All I was doing was giving you some guidance. Usually all the questioning is down to me."

Carla harrumphed and left the room.

Sara gave herself a telling off and tried to push the incident aside to deal with the staff. She went to the door and called Sandra Lang in. According to the list, Sandra was the only other female member of staff alongside Emma. A petite brunette emerged from the crowd of men hovering around the yard.

"Hello, Sandra, come through. I'm DI Sara Ramsey."

"Hi. I'm a little nervous. This has shocked me to the core."

"It's okay. I'll be gentle with you. Take a seat."

Sandra nodded and sat in the spare chair in front of the desk while Sara sat in the one Emma had vacated. Notebook at the ready, she asked, "How long have you worked here?"

"Around seven years, give or take a few months. It's not the type of job most women would plump for. I love DIY, you see. My husband and I have renovated a few houses over the years, and, well, I thought I'd put my experience to good use and apply for the job when I saw it advertised in the paper."

"Interesting. Did you get on well with Alistair Daly?"

Sandra's gaze drifted to behind Sara, and her eyes misted. "Yes, we had a laugh and joke most days."

"Was he a good employer?"

"He was the best. The type you could always go to if you had a problem. He usually had the answer to all my queries. I'll miss him. Can't believe he's gone. Ray, that's my husband, he was dumbfounded when I rang him earlier."

"It's a tragic incident, one I hope we'll be able to solve soon. Tell me, do you know if Alistair had any choice words with anyone recently?"

"Anyone?"

"Either the staff or perhaps a customer?"

She mulled the question over for a moment and then shook her head. "Not that I know of. Alistair wasn't the type to scream and shout at people. He was a very placid man. That's why all this is hard to take in. I can't believe anyone who knew him would be capable of doing that to him. Emma told us. She was beside herself. Oh God, my heart goes out to his family. His wife, his two teenage kids, what on earth will they do without him in their lives? Sorry...you don't want to hear all this."

"It's fine. It's good to be able to build a picture of the man and his life. Is there anything else you can tell me? Like how well he got on with his sister and brother perhaps?"

Sandra stared at Sara wide-eyed. "They truly were the best of friends. All three of them had a very tight bond. All laughing when they were in each other's company. I've never witnessed a cross word between them, not that Des comes in that often. No, that's wrong, he comes in a lot. What I meant was that Emma was around her brother all the time, but Des came in now and again. Oh God, am I even making any sense? Everything is there, but I'm not expressing myself very well, I'm sorry."

Sara smiled to put her at ease. "You're doing well. Please don't worry, take your time."

"Do you think someone walked in off the street and did this?"

"Possibly. We won't know that until we've spoken to all the staff. Were you working yesterday?"

"Yes, we were all here. Alistair was a stickler, expected us to get out of here within ten minutes of closing up for the trade. He was so kind and thoughtful. Never made us work later than necessary. If there was any tidying up to do, he usually stayed behind and did it. Not every boss would do that, would they?"

"No, you're right, that's unheard of. So all the staff left around what time?"

"Six o'clock or shortly after, I suppose. Five past, no later than that. We all stopped off at the pub on our way home."

"Which pub would that be?"

"The Admiral, just down the road. Sometimes Alistair and Emma join us if they haven't got any pressing family issues to attend to."

"But they didn't last night?"

"No. Emma went straight home, not sure why, and Alistair...oh God, he was going home to celebrate his wedding anniversary with Gail." She shook her head. "Oh bugger, that poor woman. She doesn't deserve this, not after what she's had to contend with this year."

Sara glanced up from the notes she was making, her interest piqued. "Meaning what?"

"Breast cancer. She had a scare three or four months ago. She's been having treatment for it, chemo or radiotherapy, I forget which one."

"Is she better now?"

"I think so. All her treatment has ended in the last month or so. They were just getting their lives back on an even keel when tragedy has struck again."

"So it would seem. How sad. And during his wife's treatment, did you notice any change in Alistair's demeanour while he was at work?"

"To others he seemed the same, putting a brave face on things, but I could tell he was concerned about his wife. He was a devoted family man; they meant everything to him."

"Okay. What can you tell me about the former employees, Martin Warman and Elizabeth Atley?"

"Nothing much really. They seemed decent enough. Martin worked here for around five years until he moved from the area. His wife's mother was ill, and they needed to relocate to Cheshire to be with her."

"And Elizabeth?"

"She was here for two years, worked mainly in the office, a secretarial role, I suppose, although she lent a hand behind the counter when we were short-staffed. She was the type who preferred to wear nail polish and refused to get stuck in properly just in case she chipped it, you know the type."

Sara smiled. "I do. Why did she leave?"

"It was all pretty sudden. Around three months ago. She told us she'd found another job. One 'more suited to her skills' was how she announced it."

Sara jotted this down. "Any idea where and what that job entailed?"

"Nope. She didn't really go into details. She didn't work her notice either. Alistair let her leave at the end of that week. Maybe she forfeited her salary so that she could start at the other job ASAP, I don't know, but that was my thought at the time."

"Okay, I'll ask Emma about the details. Is there anything else you think I should know?"

"No. I can't think of anything. I wish there was. I'll do anything to help that poor family find the person responsible for robbing us of the best boss to ever walk this earth. And no, that's not me being melodramatic. He truly was one in a million, I swear."

"With that kind of endorsement, I have a feeling our investigation is going to prove frustrating. I'll give you a card. Will you ring me if something comes to mind?"

"Of course I will. Only too happy to help. Good luck. String the bastard up when you catch him, will you?"

"I can't promise to do that, but you have my word, the guilty party will be punished to the fullest extent of the law."

"Glad to hear it. Can I go now?"

"You can." Sara gazed down at the sheet. "Can you send Paul Cox in now, please?"

"Will do. Thank you."

Sara continued making brief notes, underlining anything she felt pertinent in what Sandra had told her until a man in his forties joined her.

"Hi, you wanted to see me?"

"Hello, Paul. Take a seat. There's no need for you to be nervous. All I want to do is ask you a few questions about what goes on around here and what type of man Alistair was. Is that okay?"

"Sure. We're absolutely gobsmacked by all this. He was a good man, one of a kind. Definitely the best boss I've ever worked for. Treated everyone the same, he did. There aren't many folks that'll do that these days."

"So I've heard. Have you ever fallen out with him?"

"I've been here six years and never had a cross word with either him or Emma. That's unheard of, right?"

"I'd say so. That's remarkable. Has Alistair ever fallen out with another member of staff or customer during your time here?"

"Nope, never. That's why this has come as such a shock."

"What time did you leave work yesterday, presuming that you were here?"

"Not long after six, with the others."

"Did you happen to notice any strange vehicles loitering outside the gates, or a person walking by out there?"

"No, not that I was on the lookout for someone, sorry."

"That's okay. And all the staff went to the pub at the same time, is that correct?"

"That's right, all except Emma and Alistair. Jesus, you know what day it was yesterday for him, don't you?"

"Yes, Emma told me it was Alistair's wedding anniversary. Very sad. Has any of your colleagues ever held a grudge against Alistair?"

"No. I can't believe you'd ask such a question. I'll tell you what, for a builders' merchants, we're one big happy family. The two girls give as good as they get—you know what it's like working in a male-dominated workplace, lots of banter. We all know where to draw the line, though, nothing crude or anything like harassment, I promise. Just light-hearted banter most of the time. Alistair was always joining in, too. He wasn't the type of boss to shut himself away in the office all the time. He was part of the 'work family'."

"So I've been led to believe by Sandra. Perhaps you've witnessed an exchange of words between Alistair and a customer over the years? Anything at all?"

"Nope, can't say I have. Alistair was always able to diffuse a situation quickly with his sharp sense of humour. He was a top man and will be sorely missed. Things won't be the same around here, that's for sure."

"I feel for you. It must be tough, looking forward. I'm sure Emma will continue her brother's legacy in the same efficient manner. She's going to need all of you to support her, though."

"We'll do what we can. We all need the jobs. If we stir things up then we'll all be out on our ears. The job market is the pits these days, so I've heard from my mates. One of them has been on the dole for a few years now. Between you and me, I think he's probably got used to being a lazy bastard. Oops, sorry, that slipped out."

"Don't be. A swear word here and there often passes my lips during the course of the day. Especially when I'm dealing with a frustrating case."

"Is this going to be one of them for you?"

Sara nodded. "You could be right there. As far as I can tell, Alistair was a decent chap with no known enemies."

"Are you saying this was probably a burglary then?"

"It seems that way. Okay, if there's nothing else you can tell me, then can you give Ryan Parker the nod, let him know I'd like a quick word?"

He rose from his seat. "I'll do that. Good luck."

Sara scratched the side of her head. While she waited for the next employee to arrive, she went through her notes a second time. *Nothing, well-liked, a pleasure to work for! In that case, why did someone feel the need to torture the poor man to death? Why? And what was their damn motive?*

Sara saw the other three employees one after the other. They all basically gave the same impression of Alistair Daly. It was nearing twelve when she and Carla joined up to compare notes over a much-needed cup of coffee.

"Anything stand out for you?" she asked her partner.

"Nothing. He was well-liked, would bend over backwards to ensure his staff were happy. Doesn't strike me as the type of person people would take offence to easily."

Sara let out a sigh that puffed out her cheeks. "I totally agree. What the heck is going on then? Would someone truly walk in off the street and attack an innocent man in such a brutal way just to get their kicks and steal some money?"

"It's looking more and more likely, isn't it?"

Sara sipped her coffee. "You spoke to the assistant manager, right? Any insight from him?"

"Nope. He said exactly the same as all the others."

Sara threw her hands up in the air. "Okay, let's try and remain positive. We still have to speak to the wife yet, maybe she'll be able to shed some light on things."

Carla glanced over her shoulder and back at Sara, then leaned in. "Could the wife have paid someone to bump the husband off?"

"At this stage, I can't rule that notion out. Maybe we'll get a better feel for things once we've met her and had a chat." Something caught her eye out of the window. The next moment, Emma and Des entered the office. "Hello there, is everything all right, apart from the obvious?"

"I need a coffee before I answer that," Emma replied, marching over to the coffee machine in the corner. "Do you want one, Des?"

"Yeah, go on then, just a quick one."

Sara eyed the couple through narrowed eyes, unsure what to make of the atmosphere sparking between them. "Everything good between you two?"

"It could be better." Emma deposited the cup in her brother's outstretched hand. "He was a pain in the arse while I had to break the news to our parents."

"Hey, get real, Emma, life goes on. I have a bloody business to run. I was on my way here to pick up supplies for the couple of jobs I've got on today. I've already had to let one customer down this morning. I don't intend letting old Mrs Green down this afternoon, she's one of my best customers. I need to keep the old dear sweet."

"Bloody hell, Des, how many times do I have to say this? Your damn customers will understand in the circumstances. Alistair lost his life last night, and you're acting as though you don't care."

"That's bollocks and you know it, Em. I can't sit around here, dwelling on things. Where the hell is that going to get me, either of us, if we do that? What you need to do is get this place up and trading again. It's what Alistair would have wanted."

Sara coughed a little. "If you don't mind me interrupting your heated exchange. I can see where you're both coming from. As to opening this place, Des, Emma and her staff won't be allowed to do that until SOCO give the go-ahead. It's still a major crime scene, as I'm sure you can appreciate."

Des bashed a clenched fist against his head. "Okay, I should've thought of that. It doesn't help me, though. I need to get on with things. You can understand that, can't you, Inspector? It's not me being insensitive, I swear."

"I can understand, and if I'm honest, I think you're doing the right thing, with an added caution thrown in."

"What's that?" he asked, frowning.

"If you're a gas fitter, it's likely that your mind might drift during an installation. Have you thought about that side of things?"

"I hadn't. I'm an utter professional and can assure you my concentration levels are high when I'm at work."

"Okay, but there again, you've probably never had to deal with a murder in your family before either."

"See! That's exactly what I've been saying in the car," Emma piped up, circling her head as if her neck was knotted with tension.

"I know. I'll be fine. I promise, if I can't handle it, I'll call a halt to it and have the day off," Des told his sister. "Time is money, Em. The truth is I have a heavy bill I have to pay by the end of the month."

Sara and Carla eyed each other.

"What type of bill?" Sara asked.

Des ran a hand through his hair. "A supplier, *another* supplier is going into liquidation. I've run up a tab of over five grand, and he's given me until the end of the month to pay it."

"What? Why didn't you say something? Either Alistair or I would've helped you out."

"I don't want handouts, never have done, you know that. Bugger, I shouldn't have said anything. I need to go. I'll ring you later this evening." With that, Des stormed out of the office.

Emma closed her eyes and shook her head slowly. "Damn, what have I done now?"

"Nothing wrong as far as I can tell. Once he's had time to mull over your kind offer, I'm sure he'll apologise for throwing a wobbly."

"He's a very proud man. I'm not sure he will get used to it."

"Okay, we're about finished here. Carla and I are going to head over to see Gail now."

"Do you want me to ring and warn her?"

"Do you think that's necessary? Is she likely to be out?"

She waved a hand to dismiss the notion. "No. Sorry, I shouldn't have said that. I was only thinking of her. She might have a meltdown if the police show up at her door."

"Ah, I see. Ring her then."

Emma reached for the telephone on the desk and dialled a number. This time it seemed the smell of her brother on the phone didn't deter her from making the call. "It's Em, are you all right...? Okay, are you up to receiving visitors...? No, not me, I'm going to try and get the staff organised here... The inspector in charge of the case wants to come to see you... Okay, I'll tell her. I'll ring you later, see how things are going." Emma ended the call. "She'll be expecting you. She told me to warn you that she's a mess, though."

"That's to be expected. Thanks, Emma. Give me a call if you need me or if you think of anything which might help with our investigation. You have my card."

"I will. I don't have to tell you to do your best and catch this bastard, do I?"

"No, you don't. We'll do what we can, I assure you."

2
_____

*T*he house was out in the country at Tillington Common. It appeared to be as grand as a stately home, not what Sara had been expecting at all, although she had no reason to think otherwise.

"Wow. First of all, I didn't even know this area existed, and secondly, this is a bit grand for the owner of a builders' merchants, isn't it?" Sara asked.

Carla shrugged. "Might not have been his initially. Maybe her parents are rich and no longer with us."

"They inherited the place? Yep, totally viable to think that. Let's get in there. I hope you're prepared for a tough half an hour or so."

"Yep, I hope she's not too bad. Maybe she'll hold it together more if the kids are around."

"Let's hope so."

They stepped out of the car and approached the large Gothic-styled entrance. Sara was surprised not to see any gargoyles on the wall above.

The door opened, and a young man in a school uniform was standing there, his eyes red raw.

Sara produced her ID. "Hi, are you Ross?"

"That's right. Are you the police?"

"We are. DI Sara Ramsey, and this is my partner, DS Carla Jameson. Is it all right if we come in and speak with your mother?"

He stood behind the door and motioned for them to step inside. The hallway was as grand as the exterior—it was like stepping into a baronial hall from the seventeenth century. Sara's mouth hung open for a moment or two.

"You get used to it," Ross said. "This way."

He wound his way through the home until they reached a large kitchen, which was ultra-modern and jarred with Sara. She felt the magnificent building had been compromised.

"They're here, Mum."

Gail Daly was a slender blonde woman. Her light, checked skirt suit matched the grandeur of the house. "Hello, I'm Gail. You've met Ross, my son. This is my daughter, Lydia."

"Pleased to meet you all. I'm DI Sara Ramsey, and this is DS Carla Jameson. Let me start by saying how sorry we are for your loss. I realise how hard this must be on all of you, and please forgive the intrusion, but it's imperative we see as many members of the family as soon as possible."

"You don't need to apologise. Had you come first thing, I doubt if we would have let you in. But now, we've had time to accept my husband's death..." She gulped then sighed heavily, obviously trying her hardest to hold back the tears. "Please, take a seat. Can I get you a tea or coffee?"

Sara shook her head. "I'm fine, thank you. Carla?"

"Not for me, thanks."

Gail poured herself a coffee from the percolator sitting on the worktop and joined Sara and Carla at the table. "Are you two staying or going?" she asked her children.

"I'm out of here," Ross replied.

"Me, too. We'll leave you to it, Mum." Lydia passed by her mother and hugged her gently on her way out.

"Thank you for agreeing to see us, Gail. Is it all right if I call you Gail?" Sara began.

"Of course it is. I might live in this huge mansion; however, I'm still Gail Daly, wife to the owner of a builders' merchants. Oh dear, I should correct that, shouldn't I? You get what I mean."

Sara nodded and smiled. "I get it. You have a beautiful home. Have you lived here long?"

"Around eight years. It was derelict when we moved in. Alistair fell in love with it. He knew the owner was desperate to get it off his hands and he offered the man a ridiculously low sum for it, never dreaming the guy would accept the derisory amount, but he did. We then spent five years in total renovating it." Her enthusiasm faltered, and a sadness descended.

"You're to be congratulated, it's stunning, both inside and out."

"Thank you, that means a lot. We don't tend to get many visitors to show it off to. We're...in the process of concentrating on the grounds now. We took a year off to recover. I doubt I'm going to have the energy to take over dealing with the men Alistair commissioned to do the landscaping."

"That would be a shame. Maybe if they have the plans to go by, they won't need much input from you."

She nodded. "I suppose you're right. I'll call a halt to things while I grieve and consider what to do next in the future."

"Sounds like a good idea. No one would expect you to function normally at a time like this. Are you up to answering a few questions for us?"

"If I have to." Her head tilted to the side, and she extended her neck. "Sorry, let me sort the children out first. I can hear them arguing upstairs. It's a hard time for them." She left the table and marched to the door and shouted, "Ross, Lydia, don't think I can't hear you. Will you two pack it in and give me a bloody break. We're all hurting." Her cheeks were flushed when she returned to the table. "Sorry about that. Typical teenagers, always squabbling with each other about something or other, even at a time like this." Her hands covered her face, and she broke down. "I'm so sorry...I don't know what's wrong with me. One minute I'm fine, the next I'm a crumbling mess."

Sara patted Gail's forearm. "Please, don't apologise. Let it out, don't feel embarrassed. You've had shocking news that is life changing, it's bound to hit you at some point."

"Why Alistair? He was a lovely man with a good soul. Emma told me about the injuries he suffered. I'll never get those images out of my head, ever. Lord knows how his sister will cope after finding him like that."

"It wasn't pretty. I can get Emma some counselling, if she needs it. She only has to ask."

"I'll tell her. It sickens me that someone broke into the yard and treated Alistair like that. Had they asked for the money he had in the office, he would've handed it over, done anything to have avoided a confrontation which might, and indeed did, lead to his death. There's so much bloody violence in this world, where is it all going to end?"

"I can't answer that. All I can do is reassure you that my team and I will do everything we can to bring the person responsible to justice. I have to ask, has Alistair mentioned if he'd been confronted by anyone over the past few weeks or months?"

She gasped. "No, not at all. Do you think he was killed by someone he knew?"

"At this stage, we're unsure about that. We questioned his sister and brother, plus the other members of staff at the yard, and they all said the same thing, that the likelihood of Alistair being killed by someone he knew was unthinkable. What about the people who renovated this place? Could he have possibly fallen out with any of them?"

"No, never. We treated them as they treated us, with respect."

"Do you have a list of the people who worked for you?"

"Not really. I can give you the boss' name and phone number. He'll have to supply you with the rest."

"That would be excellent, thank you."

Gail left the table again and went in search of the information. She returned moments later carrying a sheet of paper she'd ripped from a spiral notebook and handed it to Sara.

"Brilliant. I'll give him a ring later. Is it the same people doing the landscaping? Sorry, I should've asked before you got this for me," she said, waving the paper.

"It is, at the moment. They're clearing all the land and laying the groundwork, you know, the patio and the paths, then the proper landscapers are going to come in and take over."

"I see. Okay, that makes it easier for us. What about neighbours? Has he fallen out with any of them? Possibly during the work you've had done?"

"No. Look around you. Our nearest neighbour is halfway up the lane. I don't even know who they are, to be honest."

"What about in your husband's past, anything there you can think of?"

She stretched her neck out and thought. "Not really. Before he started up the builders' merchants, he worked for another firm."

"The same line of business? A competitor?"

"Yes, but please don't say it like that. They've continued to help each other out over the years. There's never been an ounce of malice between them. Please, I can't remember Alistair speaking out about anyone, he just wasn't the type."

"That's good to know. Forgive me, I had to ask."

"Of course you did. I'm just sorry I can't help you with your investigation." She strained an ear towards the door. "Excuse me. I need to deal with the children again."

Sara nodded. This time Gail left the room and closed the door behind her.

"What are we going to do?" Carla whispered.

Sara shrugged. "It's looking more and more likely that this was a one-off, just a burglary."

Carla tutted. "I'm on the fence. How many burglaries have we investigated between us over the years that have ended in such a way? I'm getting the impression that Alistair Daly was targeted for a specific reason."

"What likely reason? The takings? They were missing after all. Or are you hinting at something else?"

"I don't really know. I'm just throwing it out there."

The conversation ground to a halt as Gail reentered the room.

"Sorry, they're struggling. Lydia needs her brother's support, and all he wants to do is sit in his room and wallow. They're both very different characters. I guess their differences are beginning to show now that they're getting older. It doesn't help me much, not at this sad time."

"Do you want me to have a word with them for you?" Sara asked, feeling sorry for the woman.

"No, I'm sure we'll cope, eventually. Was there anything else you need to know?"

"I don't think so. Would it be all right to contact you during our investigation if anything shows up and we need to clarify something with you?"

"Of course, feel free. I wish I could be of more help. I want this monster behind bars as soon as possible. I hope another family doesn't suffer the way we are at the moment. I can't believe he's gone." She broke down again.

Instead of leaving, Sara and Carla remained seated while the woman bawled her eyes out for the next ten minutes as the emotions finally swept in and took over.

Resurfacing from her grief, she dabbed at her eyes and said, "Please forgive me. I've never had to deal with a death like this before. I have no idea how I should be reacting. I've tried my hardest all morning to keep it together for the kids' sake. I don't know what came over me."

"There's no need for you to apologise. We totally understand. If I can offer a simple piece of advice, talking from experience, it's best not to bottle it up. I know everyone grieves differently, but letting your grief out will be better for you all in the long run, I promise."

"What are you saying? That you've lost a partner as well?"

"Yes. My husband. He was targeted by a gang in Manchester. He died in my arms." A lump appeared in her throat. She cleared it with a slight cough. "I had months of sitting in a cocoon, shut myself off from friends and family. It didn't help. I finally felt I had to move to a different area. I came to Hereford, and that's when the healing process began."

"I noticed the ring on your finger. Is that your husband's, or are you engaged to someone else?"

"I got engaged a few weeks ago, so did Carla to her young man. What I'm trying to say is, life goes on. I know that will be hard for you to fathom right now, but honestly, it's not an old cliché, it's the truth. I have the most wonderful fiancé now. He's everything my husband was and more."

Gail smiled. "I'm pleased for you. I can't see myself ever being happy in a relationship ever again. Alistair was a truly special man. Let's face it, there aren't too many of those left in this world. You only have to watch the news or read a newspaper to know that."

"I know. Please, hang in there, don't give up hope of finding happiness in the future, that's all I'm saying. Anyway, let the grieving process begin. There's no rush with getting on with the rest of your life. May I ask a personal question?"

Gail nodded.

"Are you financially secure? Do you have savings?"

"We have a few savings left. Alistair was insured, we both were, thank God. Not that I can think about any of that at present."

"I get that. Okay, we'll leave things there for now. Thank you for taking the time to speak with us."

The three of them left the table and walked back through the house to the front door. The children's bickering filtered down from upstairs, and Sara felt sorry for all the family, knowing the horrendous ordeal they were about to go through to get their lives back on track.

"Thank you for coming."

Sara and Carla slipped into the car before either of them spoke. Sara engaged the engine.

"I see what you did back there," Carla said.

Sara selected first gear and steered the car across the chunky gravel to the entrance. "What did I do?"

"Sneakily asked if she had life insurance."

Sara faced her partner and smiled. "It had to be asked. It's another angle we should delve into. We'll see what shows up in their bank accounts. Damn, I forgot to ask her something." Sara reversed then raced out of the car. She rang the doorbell and waited for Gail to answer it.

The woman seemed surprised to see her standing on the doorstep so soon.

"Sorry, I forgot to ask, if your husband didn't return home last night, why didn't you report him missing? Wasn't it your wedding anniversary?"

She shuffled her feet, then her sad gaze connected with Sara's. "I should have said. I've not been too well recently. Yes, you're right, it was our anniversary. We didn't have anything special planned, not really. Alistair rang me early in the day to say that he might be delayed and that he wanted to get ahead with the stocktaking. I accepted that. I'm not really one for going out on a winter's evening and I went to bed early."

"I see. Okay, thank you for filling me in."

She smiled and closed the door again. Sara ran back to the car. Carla was staring at her, waiting for the big reveal.

"I forgot to ask why she hadn't raised the alarm when her husband didn't come home last night."

"Bloody hell, I never even thought about that, and what did she say?"

"She told me they had nothing special planned and that he'd rung her earlier to tell her he was going to be working late, dealing with the stocktaking. Funny that. His sister was under the impression that he was going home to have an anniversary meal with his wife."

"How strange. Something smells off."

"Exactly. Someone isn't telling the truth. Maybe there's more to this case after all. As I said, let's look into the financial side of things and see what comes up." She started the engine again and drove back to the station.

When they walked into the incident room, they found Jill in tears being comforted by Christine. Sara rushed to see what the problem was. Her team were consummate professionals, so she knew it must be bad.

She placed a hand on Jill's back. "My God, what's happened?"

"It's Wayne. He was coming back from Dover and has been arrested." Jill bawled, and Christine took over.

"Shit, we have to help him. They found a bunch of immigrants on his lorry and have arrested him for people-smuggling."

"What the fuck? Okay, Jill, go home, you'll be no use here. Leave this with me. Who contacted you? Give me their details. I'll sort this out for you, I promise."

Christine handed a contact sheet to Sara. "It's all on there, boss. Do you want me to drive Jill home?"

"Yes, do that."

Jill got to her feet, her legs almost giving way on her.

Sara grabbed her and hugged her. "Stay strong, if only for the kids' sake, love. I've got Wayne's back. I won't allow this to happen, not to him."

Jill nodded. "Thank you," she said, her voice strained with emotion.

The door opened, and in walked DCI Carol Price, her brow curved into a frown. "I was walking past and heard the commotion. Would someone mind telling me what's going on?"

"I've just instructed Jill to go home, ma'am. Her husband has been caught smuggling immigrants on his lorry down in Dover."

"What? Tell me this is a mistake?" Price replied, clearly seething.

"No mistake, ma'am." Jill sniffled. "My Wayne would never allow people to get on his wagon. The immigrants are getting more and more desperate."

"If you're telling me he's innocent then I will do my utmost to get him off the charges. Where is he now?"

More sniffling from Jill. "He's been arrested. They allowed him to ring me, but the immigrants, they beat him up. So he's sitting in a police cell, injured. That's why I'm a mess, ma'am. To think our lot are not treating him right."

Carol Price took a few paces towards Jill and placed a hand on the top of each of her arms. "Don't worry. Leave this to me. They won't know what's hit them once I get started. Has Wayne had any bother like this before?"

"All the time. I've told him to give the job up, to only take on jobs in the UK, to stop going on overseas runs, but he says that's where the real money is. I don't care about the money. I'm worried, you know, after those thirty-nine immigrants died in the back of that lorry a few weeks back, that they'll come down heavy on him, to teach him a lesson."

"They won't, I'll ensure that doesn't happen. You go home, and I'll get on the phone straight away."

Christine hooked her arm through Jill's. "I can't thank you enough, for believing me, believing in us," Jill said, wiping her eyes with her coat sleeve.

"I have a contact for you, ma'am." Sara gave DCI Price the sheet of paper and blew out a relieved breath.

"Thanks. I'll get back to you shortly, Sara." With that, Price marched out of the room, a woman on an extremely important mission.

"Jill, now don't worry. It's best if the DCI handles this. She's got far more clout than I have. I don't want to see you back here tomorrow. Don't come back until Wayne is home again, okay?"

"What if that takes months to sort out?" Jill asked, shocked.

"It won't. Have faith. Now go. Ring me if you hear any news direct, okay?"

"I will. Thanks, boss." Jill offered the weakest of smiles and nodded at Christine. "I'm ready to go now."

"I'll be right back, boss."

"Don't rush, Christine. Make sure Jill is settled first. Will your mum be at home, Jill?"

"Yes, today is one of her days for looking after the kids."

Sara watched Jill and Christine leave the room. Shaking her head, she said, "Damn, I wouldn't want to be in his shoes, not after what's hit the headlines recently."

Carla's fingers flew across the keyboard. "I'm looking up Google now. Jill's right, these immigrants are becoming more and more desperate. Thankfully, the drivers found with the immigrants clinging on to their trucks have been treated fairly in the past. It's the ones where the people are found hiding inside locked containers, such as the thirty-nine last month, well, they're treated as people-traffickers."

"And rightly so. It doesn't alter the fact that Jill, and more importantly, her hubby, are still in a tenuous situation. Okay, that leaves us two team members down for now. Will, can you pick up the slack? Jill was digging into the financial side of things for me, can you see how far she got?"

Will nodded and moved over to Jill's desk.

"I'll be in my office if anyone needs me," Sara said, feeling deflated all of a sudden. She stopped off at the vending machine to buy herself a coffee first.

A long, arduous half an hour dragged by before Will knocked on the door, wanting a word with her. "Boss, I've got everything you asked for and a little more."

"Come in, take a seat."

He walked in, closed the door behind him and sat, his notebook in hand, ready to deliver the results of his research. "The couple's bank accounts, at first glance, appeared to be okay."

"At first glance? And once you'd taken a second look at them?"

"Okay, I sifted through their most recent statements, and everything seemed normal, the usual wages coming in, for both of them. Mrs Daly is on the payroll, too, for some reason."

"I've heard of that sort of thing going on in small businesses. Get on with it, I'm intrigued to hear what else you've found out."

"I explored further back, five to six months, and something interesting showed up on Mr Daly's statements."

She gestured for him to stop milking it.

"Back in the summer of last year, July to be precise, I noticed a few hotel stays."

Sara inclined her head. "Where?"

"In the Hereford area mostly, although one was on the outskirts of Ledbury, which is still within spitting distance of travelling home."

Sara tapped her cheek with a finger as she thought. "Too right. Not that far away that he couldn't travel home every night. Are we talking a few days, as if he was possibly attending a function or a get-together for the industry? Or are you telling me these were overnight stays?"

"I haven't had the time to find that out yet, I'll get on to it right away. I just wanted to make you aware of the situation before I went any further."

"Thanks, Will, that's very interesting. When you're asking the question, see if the room was booked in his name only."

"Are you thinking he might have been having an affair?"

Sara's nod was delivered slowly and deliberately. "It would explain why this case has been a puzzle to us so far. Everyone we've spoken to has had nothing but good to say about him. Not one person has put his integrity into question. I'm not saying these stays at the hotels aren't innocent, but the likelihood of them being the opposite is what's tapping on my mind at the moment."

"What if he was at a few functions and drank too much for him to get home the same night?"

Sara hitched up a shoulder. "Possibly. I'm going to hold off phoning Mrs Daly to check just now. You ring the hotels, get all the information you can out of them, and we'll reassess things in the morning. Time's marching on now," she said, glancing at her watch, which told her it was approaching five-thirty.

"I'll make the calls now," Will replied, exiting first the chair and then the office.

Sara picked up the phone and made the first of two calls. The first she placed to DCI Price's direct line. The phone rang and rang. She was on the verge of hanging up…

"DCI Price."

"It's Sara, ma'am. Not wishing to bother you. I was wondering how you'd got on with customs."

"I think I've sorted it. I'm waiting on a call back."

"Phew! Jill will be relieved to hear that, as am I. What did they say?"

"That Wayne was foolish, but they could tell he was innocent. They found three immigrants underneath his lorry. The men were arrested instantly. The only thing is, they took it out on Wayne and bashed him a few times. I've insisted he's accompanied to the hospital to get checked over and then released."

"Excellent news. Did they say if he was badly hurt?" she asked, doodling on her pad and writing *Yes, yes, yes* over and over.

"A few cuts and bruises. He was more in a state of shock than anything. I'm sure he'll be home either tonight or in the morning, depending what the hospital has to say in the meantime."

"I'll give Jill a ring, let her know."

"Already done. She's over the moon. Told me to pass on her thanks and to say she'll see you in the morning for her normal shift."

"She's a bloody trooper, that one. I'm glad everything has worked out for the best, for both of them. Things could've been so much worse."

"Indeed. How's the new case going? It's a nasty one, from what I've heard on the grapevine."

"Slowly. No rhyme or reason behind the man's torture so far. Saying that, Will has just stumbled across something that has piqued my interest."

"Well, what is it?"

"The man stayed in a few hotels in the area last summer."

"Hmm...business meetings? Or are you thinking more along the lines of him having an affair?"

"As we have nothing else to go on, I'm inclined to go with the latter option."

"I don't have to tell you to tread carefully, do I?"

"No, ma'am. I'll hold off questioning the wife about it for now. Will's ringing the hotels, seeing if they can share any other details with us. I'll be gobsmacked if it turns out he was having an affair, especially after everyone we've spoken to today has given us a picture of him being a wonderful family man."

"That is curious. Let's keep an open mind on that for now then."

"Will do. Are you almost finished for the day?"

"Yep, what about you?"

"Just going to head out of the door, once I've checked in with Will. It's been a long day, one I'll be glad to see the back of, I can tell you."

"Make the most of it. Once this case gets off the ground, I foresee you putting in a lot of overtime."

"You read my mind. Goodnight, ma'am."

"See you in the morning. Have a good evening."

Sara ended the first call and dialled the second number on her list. "Hi, it's only me."

"Hello, me. How are things?"

Mark's sexy voice filtered down the line. It had the strangest effect on her insides, something that had been lacking since Philip had been taken from her.

"All the better for hearing you. Are you going to be late tonight?"

"Yes, sorry. I have an emergency operation. I probably won't be home until around nine-thirty, ten o'clock time."

"That's a shame. I'll just have to snuggle up on the couch with Misty then instead."

"I'd never thought I'd be jealous of a cat. I'll try and get home earlier if I can."

"It's fine. You do what you have to do. I might even swing by Mum and Dad's on the way home. Yep, I think I'll do that."

"Misty will get jealous," he teased.

"A quick stop off. Want me to prepare you something for dinner?"

"Don't you dare. I'll grab a kebab or something on the way home."

"You eat too many of those. I can rustle up an omelette, no problem."

"Go on then, you've twisted my arm. What would I do without you?"

"Apart from starve...I really have no idea." She giggled. "See you later."

"That's true. Sara?"

She stopped herself from hanging up as his tone turned serious. "Yes, what's wrong?"

"Nothing...all I wanted to do was tell you how much I love you, that's all."

"You daft sod. I know that. See you later, you can tell me how much then."

Sara ended the call and drifted into the incident room, her steps light as if she was walking on air. Will swivelled and motioned for her to join him.

"I take it your fishing expedition has been fruitful?"

"You could say that, boss. Two of the hotels agreed to speak to me. Sadly the third refused to."

"*C'est la vie*. We can deal with that later, if we have to. I'm dying to know what you've found out."

"Our first assumption was spot on, apparently. Two people booked in under the name of Mr and Mrs Daly."

"Damn, that's not good, or perhaps it is, if it turns out to be the *real* Mrs Daly who accompanied him. My suspicious mind is telling me otherwise."

"Only one way to find out," Will replied.

"Actually, there are two ways," Sara said. "Ring the hotels back and ask them if they have any CCTV footage. We can verify who the woman is using that, rather than ask Mrs Daly the question and cause further upset to her when she's already grieving the loss of her husband. We need to tread carefully and not trample over people's feelings in a case like this."

"I'll get back to them now."

Sara walked over to the whiteboard and noted down what Will had discovered. The more she thought about it, the more she was persuaded to believe that Mr Squeaky Clean had a few dirty marks to his name after all.

Afterwards, she returned to her office and tidied up her desk. She dismissed the team and left the building with Carla, bringing her up to date on what had happened with Jill's husband during their journey.

"Crikey! Sounds like Wayne was a very lucky boy this time round. Goes to show the desperation and the lengths these people are willing to go to, to come here."

"Doesn't it? Horrendous situation when lorry drivers set off, fearing for their lives, unsure what lies in store for them once they get to the ports. I couldn't do it, live on my nerves like that."

"I hear you. Our job is a piece of piss, isn't it?" Carla chuckled, waving goodbye once she reached her car.

"Sarcastic cow. That's not what I was saying at all, and you bloody know it. Have a good one. Are you staying in tonight?"

"Yep, Gary wants me to pick out a ring from a couple of catalogues he's collected from the jeweller's in town. I'm not really in the mood, so I might try and tactfully put him off."

"You, *tactful*? That'll be the bloody day." Sara dipped into her car and pulled a face at her partner.

Carla shook her head and mouthed an expletive, and Sara roared with laughter.

She battled the traffic out of the city centre and travelled the fifteen minutes through the back lanes to her parents' place. She had decided not to ring ahead, hoping to surprise them. She wasn't bothered about her mum being upset that she hadn't had time to prepare a decent meal for her. All she wanted was to have a family chat and maybe a cuddle or two with them after her harrowing day.

"What the? How lovely to see you, darling. You should have rung. Your mother is going to be livid with you," her father said, yanking her inside out of the rain that had suddenly started lashing down.

She pecked him on the cheek. "It's only a flying visit. I didn't want Mum to go to any bother on my account."

"Nonsense. Caring for you kids is still at the top of her agenda. Your sister's in the lounge. Go through, I'll make us all a nice cup of tea."

"Coffee for me, please, Dad, not too strong." She rushed down the small hallway of the bungalow her parents had owned for donkey's years and opened the door to the lounge.

Her mother shrieked. "Sara, what are you doing here?"

"Thought I'd drop in to see how you're doing. God, Mum, it's only been just over a week since I last saw you." She leaned down to kiss her mother and then pecked her sister, Lesley, on the cheek. "What are you doing here, sis?"

"Same as you. Dropped in on the off-chance. How's work?"

"Don't ask. How are things with you now that dipshit is out of your life?"

"Sara, that's no way to speak about Lesley's former partner," her mother reprimanded.

Lesley laughed. "Mum, she's right, he was that and so much more. I'm a lot happier by myself. I guess some people are meant to go through life single, and I'm one of them."

"Don't be daft, someone new and worth knowing will drift into your life when you least expect them to. Don't give up hope, love," Sara assured Lesley.

"Not everyone is as fortunate as you in those stakes, Sara. Honestly, I'm happy as I am for now. No arguments or hassle with a significant other. The freedom to come and go at will is what I'm revelling in at the moment."

"Good for you. You seem a lot happier, I must say. Has anyone heard from Timothy lately?" she asked, enquiring after her wayward, alcoholic brother. Timothy appeared to have cut himself off from the family once he'd divorced his wife. Something that had broken her mother's heart at the time. None of them had seen Timothy's kids since the divorce. Her mother in particular was regretting not having regular contact with her only grandchildren.

"We were saying earlier that we need to get in touch with him. He's wallowed in self-pity for far too long for my liking," Lesley replied. She seemed hurt by his absence as they'd always been really close during their childhood. Sara was the middle child out of the three of them.

"I'll ring him later, if you want?" she offered as her father walked into the room carrying a tray of mugs.

"Enough about him. Are you staying for dinner?" her mother asked, struggling to get out of her soft chair.

"Sit down, Mum. No, I'm going home soon. All I wanted to do was drop in and see how you all are. How's the heart, Dad?"

He eased himself onto the sofa. "Still ticking, thank goodness."

"Has the surgery done any good?"

"I think so, dear. You don't need to worry about me. How's that young man of yours getting on? Have you discussed the wedding arrangements yet?" her father asked, swiftly changing the subject.

"He's fine. He has a late operation tonight, hence my decision to make an impromptu visit. And no, we've only just got engaged, so I don't think we'll be rushing up the aisle anytime soon."

"That's a shame, we could do with a good shindig."

"Talking about the wedding, I wanted to put your mind at ease and tell you that we'll probably be having a quiet one, nothing fancy, what with this being my second one."

"It's his first, though, isn't it?" her mother was quick to add.

"Yes, but you know what men are like. Mark's not that bothered about all the pomp and finery. He's a down-to-earth kind of guy." She glanced around the room and noticed Lesley's head drop.

Lesley was supposed to have been married by now, if that dipshit of a fiancé hadn't done the dirty on her by using the house, *her* house, as collateral against a payday loan he'd taken out with an aggressive loan shark. If Sara hadn't stepped in to sort out the situation, her sister would be back home with their parents, or worse still, homeless, by now.

She sat next to Lesley and held her hand. "Sorry, love, all this talk about weddings, it's a tad insensitive of us."

Lesley had tears glistening in her eyes when their gazes met. "Honestly, it's fine. I'm happy for you. You had it tough losing Philip like that. Which reminds me, do you ever hear from his overbearing mother now?"

Sara shook her head. "Not since I told her and her son to back off. I hated being so harsh with them, but they had become so domineering, I had to say something for my own sanity."

"Quite right, too. Philip is no longer with us. You mourned him for two years until Mark swept you off your feet. That's long enough for a young woman in her prime. My take on it is that his brother, Donald, is it?"

Sara nodded.

"I reckon he thought he was in with a chance to bed you."

"Good lord, woman, did you have to say it like that?" her father reprimanded her mother.

"Only speaking the truth, dear. Sorry if it's not what people want to hear."

"He's harmless enough, Mum. There's no way I would've ended up with him." In spite of the way she thought about her former brother-in-law, there was a time when she saw herself becoming reliant on his contact. They'd even shared a sizzling kiss, once upon a time. Something she'd regretted as soon as it happened and saw to it that it never occurred a second time. She sipped at her drink, aware of the others' gazes on her. Her cheeks warmed up.

"Glad to hear that, Sara. There's something a bit off with that one which I've never been able to put my finger on," her mother said, her eyes narrowing into tiny slits.

"Really? Why didn't you say something, Mum?"

Her mother raised her hands. "I've never really been one for interfering in my children's lives, have I now?"

Sara raised an eyebrow and glanced at her sister who shrugged. "If you say so, Mum."

"What? Are you saying that's not true?" her mother shouted, a little too loudly for Sara's liking.

It was time to make her excuses and get out of there before an argument erupted. "I'm going to say goodnight now."

"You can't do that, love, sit and finish your drink," her father insisted, seeming a little perturbed.

Sara slumped into her chair again, feeling like a scolded teenager. The conversation was a little forced, if not strained for thirty minutes, until she finally stood and said goodbye for real this time.

"Come again soon, we miss you," her mother shouted as her father saw her to the door.

"I will, Mum," she called back.

Her father hugged her. "You know how much we love you."

"I know, Dad. I need to get home, it's been a long, tiring day. All I want to do is get out of my suit and relax with Misty."

"You do that, love. Ring us if you need anything, won't you?"

"Of course." She kissed her father, gave him a final squeeze and set off down the path.

Within ten minutes, and after experiencing a hairy drive through the dark country lanes, she finally reached her home. She waved at Ted, the neighbour who had treated her like a daughter since her arrival on the new estate.

"You're late this evening. Everything all right, Sara?"

"Hi, Ted. Yeah, I'm fine. Stopped off at Mum and Dad's on the way home. How are you and Mavis?"

"I had a word with her. Can you come to us on Saturday, around seven?"

"We'd be delighted to, thank you. Saying that, I'd better check with Mark first, but I'm sure it'll be all right. He's working late tonight, an emergency operation."

"That's a shame. Give me a shout if you need anything."

"I will. Have a good evening."

She entered her home and swooped Misty into her arms. "You'd brighten the darkest day for anyone, sweetie. Are you hungry?"

Misty's loud purring was enough to tell her how excited she was to have Sara home. After changing into her leisure suit and fixing Misty some dinner, she curled up on the sofa with the adorable feline, a glass of wine and a romcom DVD.

When Mark came home she was fast asleep. His lips touched her forehead, startling her.

"Damn, what time is it?"

"Just after nine. You must've needed the rest."

"I haven't prepared your dinner yet." She struggled to her feet and staggered, momentarily feeling a touch light-headed.

Mark grasped her arm. "Sara, calm down, there's no rush. We can prepare the meal together. I take it you haven't eaten either?"

"No. I was waiting for you. I had no intention of falling asleep."

"It won't take us long. Have you had a tough day?" he asked.

Sara followed him through to the kitchen. She removed the ingredients that would need chopping up for the omelette—well, it was more like a frittata she liked to make really.

"I'll tell you about it later. Would you mind seeing to the salad?"

"I was going to suggest the same."

Once everything was prepared, the meal took ten minutes to cook and plate up. After they'd eaten and cleared up, they retired to the lounge again where she filled him in on the case.

"Blimey, that's a pretty gruesome find for someone to stumble across first thing in the morning. Awful for the sister, I bet."

"Exactly. I'm truly not sure where this investigation is going to lead us yet. It's a bit of a mystery, as they say."

He leaned over and kissed her. She tasted the red wine on his lips.

"I have every confidence that you'll break the case within a few weeks."

She smiled. "I wish I was as optimistic as you. You get a bad feeling in your gut about some cases—this is one of those. I hope we're not going to be led a merry dance."

"Positive Mental Attitude, that's the key, right?"

She chuckled. "So you have been listening to me after all."

"Cheeky. I always listen to the wise woman I share my life with."

"You're such a romantic." They united in a long kiss. "Want to go to bed?"

He extended a hand to help her up. "You go up, I'll see to Misty."

Sara ascended the stairs and jumped into bed. The problem was, she had trouble keeping her eyes open and drifted off to sleep as soon as her head sank into the pillow.

3

*M*asks in place, they left the car. They'd watched their target arrive home around nine, and through the windows, had seen the couple moving throughout the downstairs rooms. It wasn't until the light went on upstairs that they decided the time was right to put their plan into action.

They ran across the street carrying two holdalls. Luckily, the street-lights were few and far between at this end of the estate for some reason. The taller one rang the bell. They turned their backs to face the road until the door clicked open behind them.

"Hello, can I help?"

They spun around together, a well-practised movement.

The man stepped back in shock, his hand outstretched in front of him. "No, what is this? Please, don't hurt me."

Once inside the property, the shorter one closed the door behind them and attached the safety chain.

"Call her down," Tall ordered.

"No, you don't have to involve my wife in this. Do what you have to do to me, leave her out of it."

"Shut your mouth. Speak when you're spoken to and do what I say and you won't get hurt. Now, call her down."

He moistened his lips and then called out, "Jeanette, can you come down here, love?"

His wife stomped around upstairs for a few seconds and then descended the creaking staircase. When she was close to the bottom, she saw the three of them standing together and tried to flee back upstairs.

"No..." she cried as one of the masked intruders grabbed one of her legs and yanked her down on her backside. She bumped down the remaining four stairs and shouted, "Please, don't hurt us."

"Bring her in here."

The smaller one grasped Jeanette's hair and dragged her across the hallway and into the lounge where the taller one had shoved her husband.

"Tie them up," the taller of the two instructed.

Moments later, the two homeowners were sitting back to back and bound by thick rope around their chests. Shorty extracted several implements and laid them out on the carpet next to the couple.

"What's the meaning of this? Please, we've done nothing wrong. We're simple people, we can't offer you money, but there are a few pieces of jewellery upstairs. Take them if you have to," the husband said.

Tall bent down close to his face. "Shut the fuck up. This is all about revenge, mate, we're not here to rob you."

"I don't...understand. What are you talking about?"

"I told you to shut the fuck up. I hear one more word out of you, and it's your missus who'll feel the brunt of my anger, capiche?"

Their captive nodded.

"Right, now we understand each other properly, this is what's going to happen. You're going to be tortured for the sins you've committed. Any shouting out...actually, no, that's not likely to happen. Put the tape on their gobs."

Shorty unwound around ten inches of gaffer tape and slapped it on the couple's mouths.

Laughter filled the room.

"Forget what I said about not talking. You can do it now for all I care, it's not going to get you anywhere."

"Why?" Jeanette asked, voice muffled.

"All will become clear soon enough, missus, don't you worry your pretty head about that. We'll do him first. Make her suffering all the more poignant."

The guy stared down at the equipment and selected the pair of secateurs. He searched for the man's right hand and held it out, then he took his time, snipping each digit off with a slight pause in between. The man's screams were stifled by the tape. Job done, he moved on to the wife and did the same to her right hand.

Blood pooled on the carpet beneath their wounds, an unfortunate outcome. He moved on to another tool that took his fancy, a hacksaw, and proceeded to dismember the man's other hand, setting each finger on a sheet so the homeowner could see. Unfortunately, seeing the digits lying beside him, the man couldn't cope and passed out.

"That didn't take long. How long do you think you're going to last, Jeanette?"

The woman glared at him. She had spirit—he liked that in a woman. She shook her head from side to side and tried to speak. He ripped off the tape to hear what she had to say.

"You bastards. Why? What have we ever done?" She started to scream.

Tall thumped her in the face and slapped the tape over her mouth again. Then he began hacking at her wrist with the saw. She squealed and then passed out just like her husband.

"Damn, I was hoping they'd both last longer than that."

"Just get on with it. We shouldn't stay around here too long. What if one of the neighbours saw us arrive? Or worse still, heard her scream?"

"You worry too much. You choose what to do next."

"Nope, I want nothing to do with it. You do what you have to do to get your kicks, and let us get out of here."

Tall towered over his accomplice. "This is all down to you, don't ever forget that, right? Play your part or…"

"Or what? You'll do the same to me?"

He shrugged. "If the cap fits. Choose an instrument and do something."

His mate chose a hammer and travelled down the length of the man's body to his shin. Several blows rained down on the homeowner's leg until the bone crunched and shattered.

"Good, well done. Now do the same to her."

The other one continually bashed one of the woman's legs until the bone gave way. Then stood back. "That's it. We should go now."

"Why the rush? You wanted this, and now you're chickening out, why?"

"I've already said, what if one of the neighbours saw us and thinks about ringing the police?"

"I hear you. We'd better get this over and done with then. Shame neither of them is awake to see what's about to happen to them next." He picked up a small knife and stabbed the man at regular intervals across his chest. Once he'd finished with him, he moved on to the woman and did the same.

Shorty decided enough was enough and started packing up the bags.

"Hey, I ain't finished yet."

"I say we've done enough and we should make a move. I don't feel comfortable being here."

"You're a fecking wuss. All right, I think the bloke's snuffed it anyway."

"No...he can't have."

"Maybe he had a dodgy ticker. Who the fuck cares? She'll have a miserable life with those injuries. Revenge is sweet, right?"

Shorty nodded, uncertainty rearing its head. "Whatever. Let's go."

They gathered their belongings, left the tied-up couple sitting upright on the floor and flew out the front door. Shorty left the door ajar behind them. They exited the cul-de-sac quietly as if they were out on a Sunday jolly in the country.

4
_____

Sara woke and stretched. She hooked an arm over Mark and rested her head on his chest. "I'm sorry for zonking out on you last night. I must have eaten too much."

"You never have to apologise to me, love, you were exhausted, any fool could see that. Did you sleep well?"

"Straight through for a change. You?"

"Oh yes. Always sleep well when I'm snuggled up beside you."

She kissed him and threw back the quilt. "I'd better get a wriggle on. Another day has dawned in the life of DI Sara Ramsey, intrepid detective with a ton of arrests under her belt."

"You're nuts. Glad to see you're keeping your spirits up, despite being involved in a horrific case."

"I have to, otherwise I would've gone insane years ago." She entered the bathroom and ran the shower. Emerging five minutes later, she towel-dried her hair, cleaned her teeth and went back into the bedroom to find a tray sitting on the bottom of the bed. Two rounds of toast with butter and marmalade and a steaming mug of coffee. "You're the best, do you know that?" She kissed him and ran a hand down his cheek.

"You do your bit in this relationship as well."

She grabbed a slice of toast and took a chunk out of it. "We do make a pretty sensational team, don't we?"

He kissed her sticky lips then went into the bathroom. In between drying her blonde, shoulder-length hair, she ate the rest of her breakfast and was fully dressed by the time he'd gone through his morning routine. "I have to fly. Will you be back the normal time tonight?"

"Nothing booked in for late apart from the usual surgery appointments. I should be home around eight-fifteen. I'll pick up something nice from the supermarket at lunchtime, how does that sound?"

"Like an excellent idea. I'll see to Misty and be on my way. Love you, Mark."

His kiss left her breathless, making her regret it wasn't the weekend. She flew down the stairs, let Misty out in the garden, fed her and cleaned out her tray, and then called her in from the garden and secured the back door again. Moments later, she was in the car on her way to work. Luckily, she'd managed to dodge the heavy traffic by leaving a few minutes earlier and arrived at the station around eight forty-five.

She was surprised to see Jill already sitting at her desk. "Hey, you, what are you doing here?"

Jill let out a relieved breath and smiled. "Wayne came home late last night. Thanks to your intervention, boss."

Sara held up a hand. "That was down to the chief. She worked her magic. Probably threatened to get someone the sack if they didn't bloody release him. How is he?"

"Shaken up but good. I've told him to look for another job. I don't want him going through this hassle every time he takes a bloody lorry abroad, it's just not right, is it?"

"I admire any driver who risks his life in his quest to bring in a wage—that is what it's come to these days by the sound of things. He shouldn't have a problem getting another job that will keep him local, should he?"

"He's ringing a few agencies and another couple of contacts he's got today. He's not the type to sit at home twiddling his thumbs. He's a bit of a workaholic."

"You want to hang on to that one, love."

"I intend to. Anyway, I'm sure he'll get another job soon. It'll probably take him a week or two to get over his injuries, so I've told him not to go for any interviews until he feels up to it."

Sara rested her backside on the desk behind her. "Poor thing. Did the immigrants do a number on him?"

"Worked him over a little. Desperation on their part. He's lucky they didn't have a knife on them. I don't think he would be here now if they had."

"Bloody scary thought. Try not to think about that, Jill. He's safe at home, that's all that matters, believe me."

"I know. Thanks, boss."

Sara headed for the vending machine. "Coffee?"

"Thanks, that'd be lovely."

She returned carrying two coffees and glanced up when the rest of the team piled into the room together. "Shucks, sorry, guys, you're just too late. I'll be in my office if anyone needs me." She grinned and winked at the group.

Dreaded paperwork was coming out of her ears this morning. She got her head down and whizzed through it all by the time nine-thirty arrived.

There was a knock on her door, and Carla poked her head into the room. "Just had a call that I think we should attend."

"Come in, tell me what it is?"

Carla sat in the chair opposite and heaved out a sigh. "I'm thinking it's connected to the Daly case."

"What is? Come on, partner, you're going to have to do better than that."

"Yesterday you asked me to interview half the staff while you questioned the rest."

"Yep, I remember. Can you get to the point before I lose the bloody will to live?"

"Sorry. Well, on my list of staff to interview was the assistant manager, Bob Lockett."

"And?"

"Well...he's now dead."

Sara shot out of her chair, tipping it back in the process. "What? Where? Was it intentional or an accident?"

"I'd say it was bloody intentional all right. At home. That's not all. His wife was tortured as well."

"Shit, damn and blast. Are they both dead?"

"The wife survived. She's in hospital."

"That's a relief. But the husband is dead? Both tortured? This can't be a bloody coincidence, can it? Okay, get your coat on, we're going over there."

There were several patrol vehicles already at the scene when they pulled up outside the couple's detached home at the end of the cul-de-sac. It was a nice area, nothing special compared to his boss' residence. Sara and Carla got suited and booted and then flashed their IDs to the uniformed officer at the front door.

"Lorraine, are you here?" Sara called.

"In the lounge on the right. You'll want to see this one."

Sara followed Lorraine's voice and eased open the lounge door. "Jesus, what the fuck?"

Carla peered over her shoulder and said virtually the same, except she left out the Jesus part.

The two of them entered the room.

Sara could already sense her breakfast threatening to make a reappearance. "Who found him, I mean them?"

"Apparently, whoever did this carried out the deed and then left the front door ajar on their way out."

"That's interesting. So they intended for the couple to be found quickly then."

"Yep, that's my take on it. I sent the woman off to hospital, she was a mess." Lorraine pointed at some fingers lying on a sheet near the man's body. "Those are his. She had all hers cut off, too. I bagged them up with some frozen peas and sent them with her. I'm not raising my hopes on whether the surgeons can work their magic or not, though."

"Damn, why's that? Or is that a dumb question?"

"Pretty dumb. Time is of the essence with missing limbs or body parts. They already looked dead to me. They'd been lying there for possibly around eleven hours before we showed up. Depending on the way they were dismembered, there's a time limit of between six and twelve hours. My thinking is that they're too far gone to think about surgically reattaching them."

"Seriously? There's a time limit on things like that? I had no idea, although thinking about it, logic tells me there ought to be. Poor woman. Did she say anything?"

"She was very weak. The bloody ambulance took ages to get here. I had to comfort her." Lorraine cringed. "You know how shit I am at doing that sort of thing with people who are still breathing."

Sara rolled her eyes. "You're unbelievable."

"What? I'm speaking the truth. All my words of comfort come to those who've already passed."

"Okay, you don't have to fill me in further, I get your drift. What did she tell you, anything of interest?"

"Oh plenty, only I'm too busy dealing with her dead husband. I suggest you call at the hospital and have a word with her yourself."

Sara tutted. "Who's rattled your cage?"

"No one. I'm up to my eyes in things here, in case it has slipped your notice."

"It hadn't, but thanks for tactfully reminding me, not!"

Lorraine took her foul mood out on her team, ordering them to photograph the victim and to arrange for the stretcher to move the body, while Sara motioned for Carla to join her in the hallway.

"Always best to steer clear when she's got one on her."

"That's strange, I hadn't picked up on anything until you mentioned it. Guess I don't really know her as much as I thought I did."

"You have to look at her eyes. They emit a warning sign like no other pathologist I've ever worked with. Anyway, enough about Mardy Pants in there, we have work to do."

"Like going to the hospital?"

"Eventually. I think we should hang around here for now to question the neighbours. My take is the woman will need emergency surgery once she reaches the hospital. We're not likely going to get any sense out of her for a few hours yet, agreed?"

"You're right as usual. Do you want to take one side and I'll do the other?"

"Why not? Makes sense to me. Ask the usual thing, what they saw, any strange vehicles on the close. Did they hear anyone either scream or cry out for help? You know the drill."

Carla shook her head. "I do, but thanks for the recap on procedures."

Sara pulled a face. "Don't you start, I've got enough hormone-related hassle from that bitch in there."

"Sorry, okay. I'm off."

They split up, heading in different directions in the cul-de-sac.

The first house Sara knocked at revealed an elderly couple in their eighties. "Hello there. I'm DI Sara Ramsey. We're conducting enquiries in the area. I wondered if I might have a quick word with you both."

"Come in out of the cold, dear. We've got the gas fire on in the lounge," the husband said.

The smell of menthol followed the elderly couple down the narrow passage and into the first room on the right. There was indeed a gas fire lit, glowing brightly, taking the chill off the relatively large room.

"You sit down there, love," the wife instructed.

Sara sat and withdrew her notebook and pen from her pocket. "Thank you, you're very kind. Obviously, you're aware of an incident happening at the Locketts' residence. What I'm trying to do is build a picture of the events. Did you hear or see anything last night?"

"No, Wilf and I were in bed quite early. The first we knew of anything being wrong was when Wilf took Tootsie out for her walk around eight." She pointed to a tiny Yorkshire terrier curled up in a comfy bed on the other side of the fire which Sara hadn't even noticed when she'd walked into the room.

"I see. That's a shame."

"Can you tell us what's happened to them? Jeanette and Bob are such a nice couple. If anything bad has gone on there...well, it would be a great pity," Valerie asked, holding tightly to her husband's hand.

"It would. Nice couple. The type who'll bend over backwards to help their neighbours out. We had problems with our water heater only last week, and Bob took it upon himself to sort the damn thing out for us. I wasn't hinting, he insisted he knew what the problem was. He fixed it and refused to take any money from us. He's a real gent, that one," Wilf said.

Sara smiled and exhaled a large breath. "I'm sorry to have to tell you that Bob lost his life in an attack."

"Oh no, that can't be right, not Bob," the wife screeched, clinging to her husband's hand even tighter.

"It's all right, Valerie, hush now. Let the police officer speak, dear," Wilf said, shaking his head in disbelief. "What about Jeanette, was she hurt?"

"Yes, she's on her way to hospital. I'm unsure as to the extent of her injuries until I see her myself. May I ask if you've noticed anyone or a strange vehicle in the close over the past few weeks?"

The couple glanced at each other, all the colour drained from their wrinkled faces. They shook their heads.

"No, can't say we have, dear, sorry," Wilf replied on behalf of his wife.

"Okay, then I need to move on to see what your other neighbours can tell me. Please, I want to assure you not to worry about this incident."

"How can you say that?" Wilf demanded, rising from his seat on the sofa.

"Because I believe the Locketts were intentionally targeted. I'm already investigating a similar case."

"And that's supposed to reassure us?"

Sara shrugged. "Sorry, maybe I shouldn't have mentioned it. I just wanted to put your mind at ease."

"I see. Okay, I get where you're coming from now. Although, your reassurance isn't going to make the situation any better, I promise you," Wilf assured her, opening the door to the lounge and disappearing into the hallway.

Sara patted Valerie on the shoulder and then followed her husband to the front door.

"I wish you hadn't said that," Wilf whispered, leaning forward. "She's going to be petrified now, mark my words on, she's a right worry guts."

"I'm so sorry. Please, there's nothing for you to be worried about. I'm going to ensure a patrol car comes to check the area frequently over the next few days."

"And then what? When all the fuss has died down, who'll bother about us then?" Wilf's eye twitched at the side, displaying how annoyed he was.

Sara smiled weakly, unsure how to put the man at ease. Nobody could at this stage because, in truth, they didn't know what they were dealing with, except the killer or killers were brutal and dangerous. "Thank you for your time, sir."

He grunted and opened the door. She stepped out and the whoosh of a draught came from behind her as she left. *And a very good day to you, too.* Sara blew out a frustrated breath and glanced across the cul-de-sac to see how Carla was doing. By the stormy expression on her face, she concluded her partner was matching her lack of success. She waved and gestured that she was moving on to the next house. Carla gave her the thumbs-up and did the same. Within half an hour, between them they had spoken to all the residents, most of whom couldn't tell them anything.

The exception to the rule was an old lady called Moira. She was the one who had discovered the couple and was beside herself with grief. Her son, Aiden, had turned up and was at the house comforting her. Moira had explained how she'd nipped out to put something in her recycling bin and noticed the Locketts' door was ajar. She never dreamed she'd see her dear friends in that state. Again, she hadn't seen anything untoward going on in the cul-de-sac, not that she could remember.

Sara and Carla got back in the car, both of them ticked off by their lack of clues.

Sara bashed the steering wheel with her fist. "You'd think someone would've seen something, wouldn't you?"

"They're all elderly, apart from the Locketts. I suppose it was to be expected. On the other hand..."

Sara turned to face her partner. "Go on?"

"It could tell us that the person or persons we're dealing with are professionals."

"Professionals, as in hitmen? Is that what you're implying?"

Carla frowned. "Why is that so hard to believe?"

Sara hitched up a shoulder. "It's not. The suggestion just floored me." She fired up the engine. "Off to the hospital. Let's hope Jeanette can tell us more than her neighbours have between them."

Carla dipped down and looked at the sky. "Is that a pig flying?" She sat back in her seat and added, "My guess is she's going to be so traumatised she's going to struggle to tell us anything."

"Perhaps. She probably won't be compos mentis for a few hours after the surgery takes place."

"Do we have time to stop off and have a coffee and a cake then? Or is that wishful thinking on my part?"

"Your wish is my command. Want to stop off at Morrisons, that's close to the hospital, right? We could leave the car there and walk the rest of the way."

"You seem to have it all worked out."

Sara headed back into town and parked up in Morrisons. They rushed in and chose a cream doughnut and a latte each.

"Sod the calories, we'll probably end up going without lunch today, so why not?"

Carla smiled and wiggled her eyebrows. "Yum, a cream cake, a mortal sin that has to be committed now and again."

"You forgot to add, not only to satisfy cravings but also to help conquer a trying day, which I believe this is going to turn out to be."

"You're not wrong there. Why? Why do you think someone is going around torturing people?"

"More to the point, why have they specifically targeted a couple of work colleagues? Damn, that reminds me, I'd better ring Emma to make her aware of what's happened before she hears it on the news."

"That's going to come as a shock to her after her brother's death."

"Isn't it just?" Sara gobbled a mouthful of cake and chewed it vigorously as she dialled Emma's mobile number.

"Hello."

Sara swallowed a large lump of doughnut. "Hi, Emma. This is DI Ramsey, are you sitting down?"

"Oh God, don't say that. Have you caught the bastard?"

"Sorry, not yet. Umm...I need to break some more bad news. Are you sitting yet?"

"I am now. You're scaring me. What is it?"

"I'm afraid Bob Lockett and his wife were targeted last night at their home."

"Oh no, I can't be hearing this. I wondered why he hadn't come into work this morning. Why? Oh God...they're not dead, are they?"

Sara puffed out a breath she'd been hanging on to. "Sadly, Bob didn't survive. We're on our way to visit Jeanette in hospital now."

"Is she bad? Oh, heck, those poor people. Were they subjected to the same thing as Alistair?"

"It's hard to distinguish which crime was worse. I suppose we have to be thankful that Jeanette has survived. Hopefully, she'll be able to tell us who attacked her and her husband, eventually."

"Eventually? What do you mean by that, Inspector?"

"She's suffered bad injuries that will need surgery."

Emma remained silent for a few seconds and then sniffed a little.

"Emma, are you all right?"

More sniffling. "Yes, oh shit, I'm a mess. What does this all mean? Are any of us safe?"

"Honestly, I can't answer that. Can you stay with someone, is that possible?"

"Yes, I think so. What about this place? Should I carry on trading? What if the bastard shows up here again?"

"My advice would be to carry on trading but to ensure that no one is left alone at the premises when locking up. Can you manage that?"

"Yes, I think so. Oh God, poor Bob. The staff are going to be devastated when I tell them. Please, send my regards to Jeanette. We'll organise a collection. Tell her I'll visit her soon."

"Take care of yourself, Emma. You're still grieving the loss of your brother, don't overstretch yourself." Sara toyed with her doughnut, temptingly sitting on the plate in front of her.

"I decided to come in today, it's what Alistair would've wanted. His mantra was always 'the show must go on'. I'm trying to stick to that, although hearing what's happened to Bob and Jeanette, well, you can imagine the emotional state I'm in right now."

"I can. Be gentle on yourself, Emma. Is there someone else who could take over from you?"

"No, that would have been Bob's job. Shit! How the hell are we going to cope around here with both of them gone?"

"You'll cope, I have every confidence in you. It might take a little time, but you'll get there."

"Thank you for informing me. I'll go and let the rest of the staff know. Please, do your best, Inspector."

"You have my word on that." Sara pushed the rest of her cake away, suddenly feeling guilty for stopping off at the café. She stabbed the End Call button and stared out of the window.

Carla slid her cake back in front of her. "Eat it. I know you don't feel like it, but you're going to need it to keep your strength up for later."

"I know what you're saying makes sense but I doubt I'd be able to keep anything down. Shit, what have these poor people done to deserve being tortured to death?"

Several people sitting on the nearby tables turned her way.

Sara's cheeks heated and she issued an apology. "Sorry, folks, just going over my lines for a play, nothing to be concerned about."

The other customers either grinned or nodded, accepting her excuse.

"That was quick thinking," Carla whispered.

"A brainstorm, right?"

"I wouldn't go as far as that." Carla smirked and continued to tuck into her wicked temptation.

"Want mine as well?"

"Nah, one is my limit."

"I'll stick to the coffee. We'll have this and trek over to the hospital. We've got two hours on the clock before we have to shift the car."

"It's better than paying the hefty charge at the hospital. Last time I parked in there I nearly had to take out a second mortgage to cover the damn fee. Five quid for just over an hour it was, bloody scandalous."

Sara giggled. "Have you heard yourself?"

Carla pulled a face that made her look like a constipated rabbit. "I'm entitled to whinge, it's in my nature."

Sara finished the rest of her drink and urged Carla to do the same. She was eager to get on with her day rather than debate the rights and wrongs about the excessive parking charges in Hereford.

Minutes later, after a brisk walk through the street leading up to their destination, they entered the main hospital entrance. At the reception desk, Sara showed her ID and asked the brunette behind the counter where they were likely to find Jeanette Lockett.

The woman tapped at her keyboard and smiled. "Ah, here she is, on the second floor, the surgical ward."

"Thanks, is there a lift somewhere?"

"Along the corridor and on the right."

Sara nodded her thanks. They jumped in the lift that was kindly waiting for them and emerged on the second floor. Sara again showed her ID once they were on the ward. "Is it possible to have a word with Jeanette Lockett?"

"Not right now, no. She hasn't come around from her operation yet," the nurse on duty replied.

"I thought as much. Is that going to take long?"

"A good couple of hours. My suggestion would be to go away and come back later."

"If it's all the same to you, this is a very important inquiry, and we need to speak to her as soon as she wakes up."

"That's up to you. I'm going to have to put my foot down and say you'll have to wait outside then. She's in a private room, and I don't want her to be disturbed."

"Fair enough. Will you come and get us as soon as she wakes up?"

"I will." The blonde nurse shuffled the papers in front of her as if to dismiss them.

Sara took the hint and nudged Carla. They made themselves comfortable in the seats outside the ward.

"I'm going to check in with the team." Sara rang the station, and Will answered the phone. She explained the situation and asked if he had any news.

"As it happens, yes, ma'am. I was about to ring you."

"Sounds ominous. Go on."

"The hotels got back to me with the CCTV footage. They show Alistair Daly with his arm around a redhead who seems to be in her twenties."

"Have you got an image you can send me? It definitely doesn't sound like Mrs Daly to me, she's blonde."

"Sending it through now."

Her text message jingle went off. "Just a sec, I'll have a peek." Sara opened the text and gasped. "Bloody hell." She angled her phone for Carla to take a look.

Carla tutted and shook her head.

Sara raised the phone to her ear again and said, "Will, I can confirm that is *not* Mrs Daly. Not the Mrs Daly we've spoken to."

"As we thought, he must've been having an affair then, ma'am."

"Indeed, but who with? Who is this damn woman and, more to the point, does she have anything to do with his death?"

"What do you want me to do now, boss?"

"Run her through the system, if you would. See if facial recognition throws up anything."

"Doing it now. I'll get back to you if there's a hit."

"Okay, I've got no idea how long we're likely to be here. See you later." She ended the call and paced the hallway. "Could a woman truly be responsible for his murder?"

Carla shrugged. "Sounds as if that's likely. Maybe she had an accomplice. We've yet to establish that."

"Still, it's all rather perplexing. What gets to me is that everyone painted this picture of him being a goody-two-shoes. The best husband and father to ever walk the earth, when all the time he was having an affair. Things don't stack up to me."

"Me neither. What do you propose doing about that?"

"What can I do? Haul everyone we've spoken to so far into the station and ask them what they're playing at?"

"Why not? It might be our only chance of getting to the truth."

Sara circled the floor, dwelling on that notion for the next five minutes. She grunted. "I'll tell you one thing, my ex-DCI would be doing just that right now, to get to the bottom of things."

"Seriously?"

"Yep." Sara flung herself into one of the plastic chairs. "I'm bloody bored already. Hate hospitals at the best of times, but to be here now, forced to hang around like this is going to drive me nuts."

"You go, leave me here. It doesn't bother me as much as it does you, apparently."

"Nah, I'm allowed to bellyache now and then, just ignore me. I wonder how long we're going to have to wait."

"It depends on how bad her injuries are. I'm guessing at least another three to four hours."

"Gee, thanks. I was hoping you'd be more on my side and say around two, max."

"Why hang around then? We could be revisiting those we've already spoken to and get the ball rolling into the Locketts' backgrounds."

Sara fished her phone out of her pocket. "Well, there's nothing stopping me from initiating the latter from here." She contacted the station again, and this time Christine answered. "It's me again. It looks like Carla and I are going to be tied up at the hospital for the best part of the day. I need you guys to start doing the background checks on the Locketts for me."

"Will do, boss. Are we searching for anything in particular, or just general bits and bobs?"

"The usual. My brain is whirling all the time, so don't be surprised to hear from me again soon. Good luck, Christine."

"Thanks, boss. I'll let you know if I find anything."

Sara ended the call and leaned her head back against the wall. Her mind racing, she ran through everything they had to date on the two cases and sat bolt upright. "Damn!"

"What's wrong?"

"Why didn't I think of it as soon as Will sent me the photo? The woman...I'll see if Emma knows her. She could be a customer at their gaff, who knows?"

"Umm...maybe now isn't the right time to be bothering her, you know, what with her being in shock, the second day in a row."

"Nonsense. We need to get to the bottom of this, and quickly. The sooner I get in touch, the sooner we'll possibly have a name to work with."

"Whatever. I don't need to tell you to be careful, do I?"

"No, you don't. Although, I must say, I'd rather go see her myself than do it over the phone. Such is life." She dialled Emma's number. "Hi, Emma, it's Sara Ramsey again. Sorry to bother you so soon. Something has come to my attention, and I'm wondering if you could shed some light on it for me."

"I'll do my best," she replied uncertainly. "What do you need?"

"We've stumbled across video footage of Alistair with a woman. After meeting his wife yesterday, I know it's not her. I wondered, if I sent you the image, whether you'd have a shot at identifying her for me."

"A woman? Where?"

Sara sighed. "The footage was taken at a hotel here in Hereford."

"Were they having lunch?"

"I'm not sure what they were up to. Umm...I'm hoping the image doesn't upset you too much."

"What's that supposed to mean?"

"All I'm saying is they seem a touch friendly in the shot."

"Jesus…okay, send it through."

Sara glanced up at Carla and rolled her eyes. Then she sent the image via text and held the phone to her ear to listen to Emma's response.

"For fuck's sake…"

"Emma, do you know her?"

"You could say that."

"Who is she? Were they having an affair?"

"Elizabeth Atley, and yes."

"Where do I know that name from?" Sara asked, her brow aching from her deep frowning.

"She was on the list of names I gave you. She was on the previous employees' list."

"Okay. I'm confused. Who knew they were having an affair?"

"Everyone here knew."

Sara gritted her teeth and thumped her thigh. She inhaled and exhaled a few times to try to calm herself down, fearing she was about to explode at the woman. "And none of you thought to mention it?"

"No. The affair ended when she left the firm a few months ago. Personally speaking, I'd rather forget about the bitch."

"Seriously? You're calling her a bitch now and yet you never thought to tell me about their affair? What were you thinking when I questioned you as to whether Alistair had fallen out with someone recently? I can't believe what I'm hearing. This is a damn murder inquiry, a double one now, and yet a dozen or more people chose to keep quiet about this blasted affair. Can you see what I'm getting at?"

"I'm sorry. I get that now. In my defence, I was in shock at finding my brother."

"Okay, that much I can understand, sort of. Tell me, did Gail know he was having an affair?"

"Yes. Alistair called a halt to seeing Atley the second Gail started her treatment for breast cancer. He saw it as a sign of punishment."

Sara shook her head, not believing the sudden turn the investigation had taken. "A punishment? He thought God was punishing his wife for him having an affair?" Sara was gobsmacked by the logic to that absurd notion.

"Yes. He was a churchgoer."

"Seriously? And no one thought to mention that either? He cheats on his wife and has the audacity to attend frigging church?" The words were set free before Sara had the chance to stop them spilling out.

"Yes. We've all sinned in this life, Inspector, or are you telling me you've never gone against God's wishes?"

"I refuse to answer that, Emma. My religious beliefs have nothing whatsoever to do with this investigation. I'll tell you one thing. You and your colleagues have genuinely compromised this investigation from the outset."

"I'm sorry you think that way."

"Choosing to keep Alistair's affair a secret has undoubtedly contributed to Bob's death and to his wife suffering severe injuries that she may never recover from. I hope you're pleased with yourselves."

There was silence on the other end. Sara realised she'd been harsh on the woman, but she had to get it through to her, and her workforce, how much their evasive answers had damaged the investigation.

"Are you still there?" she prompted.

The sniffling started up again. "I'm here. What can I tell you? Except to say I'm sorry. I did it because I was in shock and didn't want to speak ill of the dead."

"Okay, we'll leave it there. I need to tell you that your deceit, all of you, has severely hindered this investigation. One last thing before I go."

"I can't keep apologising, Inspector. In our defence, we're all grieving the loss of a good man. Whether he had an affair or not, he was still a lovely person."

"I get that, I think. How likely is it that Atley is still at the same address? Has anyone heard from her since she left the firm?"

"No, as far as I know she hasn't been in touch with anyone here. I'm sure they would have mentioned it. You'll have to go there. I don't know if she's remained at the same flat or not."

"What about references? Did either you or Alistair give her one? Has a potential employer been in touch for a reference since she left?"

"Alistair gave her a reference. He let her leave at the end of that week. We usually expect our staff to work a month's notice. Her departure was handled differently."

"Because of the affair?"

"Yes."

"Okay, I'll be in touch if I need any other information. And, Emma, if you could be honest with me going forward, it'll make my life a whole lot easier." Sara jabbed at the End Call button before Emma could respond. She banged her head against the wall behind her repeatedly until Carla grabbed her arm.

"Stop that. Don't you dare go blaming yourself, Sara."

"I can't believe what that damn woman has just told me. Of all the…ugh…what is wrong with people? These two were having an affair, and no one, I repeat, no bugger thought to tell us? Well, once the news comes out about Bob and Jeanette, I hope they're damn well pleased with the part they've played in the couple's misfortune or demise."

"You need to calm down. They probably thought they were doing the right thing by not saying anything."

Sara sharply turned to face her. "Are you for real? This is a frigging murder investigation. I know damn well if I was aware of a victim having an affair, I'd shout about it to the investigating officers."

"That's because you have a police brain. Grief affects people in different ways. We have to make allowances for that."

"Maybe if we're talking about one or two people, I'd be able to accept that, Carla, not what, thirteen of them, for fuck's sake? I'm livid about this. When people are stupid about the information they give us, then I just want to throw my hands up in the air and say, 'Hey, guys, if you can't be arsed, then neither can I'. Makes me so frigging irate."

"Because if you did that, you're the one who would likely get into bother for it, not them. You can't think like that, Sara. You need to try and calm down and think about this rationally."

Sara seethed, and her cheeks heated before she finally blew out a steadying breath. "You're right. Getting worked up about it isn't going to get me anywhere. Who made you the sensible one in this partnership anyway?"

Carla winked at her. "I'm only telling it as it is. Had you taken a step back you would've said exactly the same to me if I'd gone off on one. I'll grab us both a coffee." She left her seat and wandered down the hallway to find a vending machine.

Sara rang the station again, for the third time since they'd arrived. This time Marissa answered her call. "Hi, it's me. Is Will there?"

"I'll put him on, boss."

Will came on the line. "I'm here, boss. What's up?"

"The woman at the hotel, I have a name for you. Elizabeth Atley, she's on the former employees' list."

"Shit! Okay, what do you want me to do?"

"Find out if she's still living at the same address, and if so, where she's working now. I need to have an urgent chat with the woman."

"Right. You think she could be behind the murders?"

"I can't rule her out at this stage. My thinking is that she was asked to leave her job because of the affair, and that would give her a decent motive, yes?"

"I'm inclined to agree with you. Leave it with me. I'll ring you as soon as I find out anything."

"Thanks, Will. I'll be sitting here, waiting for your call."

He laughed and hung up. She sat there for a few minutes.

Carla returned and handed her a cup.

"Great. I hope we don't have to stay around here too long now, I'm chomping at the bit to get on." Sara's mobile rang. It was Will.

"Hi, boss. No go, I'm afraid. I managed to track down her landlord. She moved out a couple of months ago. He was livid; she owed him a couple of months' rent. There one day and the next gone, was how he put it."

"She sounds a nice lady, doesn't she?"

"Would that make her a killer, though, boss?"

"At the moment, I'm going to cling on to that thought, Will. Let's face it, we've got fuck all else to go on. I don't suppose the landlord mentioned where she was working now?"

"I tried to get it out of him; he said he didn't know."

"Helpful, not! Okay, we'll get back to the bum-numbing task of hanging around here then. Speak later."

"Have fun."

*T*hey had to contend with another three more hours of boredom until the sister of the ward came to fetch them.

"Inspector, Mrs Lockett is awake now."

Sara shot out of her chair. "Is she up to speaking with us?"

"I've asked her. She's desperate to see you. I must warn you to take things easy with her."

"You have my word."

They followed the sister back through the swing doors and into the private room close to the entrance. Jeanette was sitting up in bed, her hair messy, looking decidedly groggy. Which didn't bode well in Sara's eyes.

"Hello, Jeanette, how are you feeling?"

Jeanette held out her two arms which Sara could tell were nothing more than stumps. "How do you think? They couldn't save my fingers or my hand." Her voice was fraught with emotion—to be expected.

Sara approached the left side of the bed and laid her hand on the woman's shoulder. "I'm sorry, I'm sure the surgeons did their best in the circumstances."

"It wasn't good enough. How am I going to cope without hands and without my husband to help me? They told me Bob had died…" A sob cut her off.

"I'm sorry for your loss and for the pain and suffering this person caused you."

"*Persons*, plural, there were two of them. The gutless cowards wore masks. I'll never be able to identify the bastards who have dramatically changed my life."

"Two, are you sure?"

Jeanette faced her and glared. "Of course I'm sure. I might have just had surgery, but there's nothing wrong with my memory. My anger has seen to that. Why? Why did these people burst into our home and feel the need to attack us in such a brutal way?"

"We've yet to establish that, Jeanette. Did either of your attackers give you any hint as to who they might be, or perhaps let anything slip, like a name or why they chose your house?"

"No, I would have told you if they had."

"What time did they arrive? Can you remember?"

"Yes, I was on my way up to bed at ten. The bell rang, and Bob answered the door. Why did he do that? At that time of night? If only he'd ignored it, maybe he'd still be here today and I wouldn't be facing a life of disability." Fresh tears sprang to her eyes.

"Please, try not to upset yourself."

"Upset? Upset? I'm bloody livid. Worse than that, angry beyond words that someone walked in off the street and tortured us like that. We're good people. Never done anything to hurt anyone else in this world and yet…"

"I know. I have to tell you that we're treating this investigation as part of our ongoing case, the murder of Alistair Daly."

"I kind of figured as much for myself. What I can't get my head around is why. Alistair was a decent chap. Did right by the staff and his family. Always treated me and Bob well over the years. Why would anyone choose to torture us? It's not as if they tried to get any information out of us. Yes, they wore masks, but I could tell they were enjoying what they were doing. It wasn't as if they were having second thoughts about being there. Oh God, I'm worn out. This has taken its toll on me. I thought I was strong enough to speak to you but I'm not. Please, I want you to go now."

"If that's what you want. One last question, if I may?"

Jeanette nodded and rested her head back against the pillows propped up behind her.

"The intruders, do you have any idea what gender they were?"

Jeanette frowned. "No. I presumed they were both men. Is there some kind of doubt about that?"

"No, not at this stage. I'm merely asking the question, trying to fit all the pieces together. Thank you for speaking with us. I hope you're on the mend soon." Sara mentally kicked herself for sounding so blasé. What did you say to someone in Jeanette's position, with nothing in her life to look forward to except living with a great deal of pain and discomfort?

Jeanette closed her eyes and drifted off to sleep. Sara and Carla left the room and reported back to the sister.

"She's resting now. All right if I leave a card with you? If she thinks of anything, will you make sure she contacts us?" Sara gave the woman a card.

"I'll do that. Her son is due in soon. I'll pass your card on to him, if that's all right?"

"That'd be fantastic. Look after her."

The sister nodded. "We'll do our very best for the poor woman. Hopefully you'll soon find whoever did this to her."

Sara held her crossed fingers up and smiled. "That's the plan. Thanks for allowing us to see her. I appreciate it."

Once they were in the lift, Carla asked, "Back to the station?"

"Nope, I want to call in and see how Gail is doing, or rather try and get to the bottom of why she felt the need to hide her husband's affair from us."

5

*G*ail opened the door to them swiftly once they arrived at the house. "Do you have some news on my husband's murder?" Her gaze darted between them expectantly.

"Would it be okay if we came in for a few minutes, Gail?"

"Of course, I'm sorry." She scooted back behind the door and gestured for them to step inside. Then she led them through the vast house to the kitchen at the rear where their initial interview had taken place.

"Please sit down. What news do you have for me? Have you arrested the killer? Do you know who it is? I apologise, I'm eager to know. Life has been hell since his death."

"I understand your eagerness. No, we're no further forward with the case."

"What? Why not? Why are you here?"

In the car, during the journey over there, Sara had prepared herself for what she was about to say next. She placed her hands on the table in front of her. "The truth is that our investigation was hampered from the beginning, and it has proved to be detrimental."

Gail frowned, and she tilted her head. "Hampered? In what way?"

"By Alistair's family members hiding a grave secret from us."

Gail's gaze dropped to the table, her shoulders slumped, and she fell back in her chair. "You're talking about the affair, aren't you?" she muttered.

"Why didn't you tell us? Oh, and don't worry, I've had the same conversation with Emma about this. Why?"

"It was over. As soon as I found out about the breast cancer, he ended it. Life has been pretty damn good for the last few months. All things considered with the treatment I've had to endure. Why would I bring the affair up?"

"You all painted Alistair to be the kindest of men, and it's that impression that stuck with us. It put a different spin on our investigation. We couldn't figure out why someone he knew would have tortured and killed him, therefore, we went down the route of this being a burglary of sorts, a one-off that went tragically wrong."

She gasped. "I see. Oh my, I never meant for that to happen. You're not saying that…"

"I don't know what I'm saying yet, but given that we've only just discovered that your husband had an affair, we've been forced to begin our investigation again."

"Are you telling me you think *she* killed my husband?"

"I'm not saying anything of the sort. Let's just say she's a person of interest. I need to know if either you or your husband have ever received any form of threat from Elizabeth Atley."

"I haven't. I'm not sure if Alistair had in the months since he ended the affair. Do you know where she lives?"

"Do you?" Sara retorted, picking up on the way Gail had asked the question.

"I sat outside her flat one day. I was desperate to go in there and have it out with her…"

"But?"

"I hesitated long and hard and eventually decided she wasn't worth it. I had my husband back, and my family was complete once more. I did the right thing and drove away."

"Did your husband ever tell you why he started the affair in the first place?"

She took her time to answer, chewed on her lip for a few moments. "What type of question is that?" she snapped eventually.

"I'd say it was a pretty pertinent one in the circumstances." Sara clenched her hands tighter together, trying to relieve some of the tension running through her.

"Why do men usually end up having affairs?" Gail shouted, tears dripping onto her cheeks.

"Just answer the question." Sara was losing her patience with the woman who had already tried to deceive her.

"Because he was bored. Bored with me and the life we had together." Her chin dipped onto her chest.

"But you overcame all that and were able to start over again, is that right? Or is there something else you're keeping from me?"

"No. That's all."

Sara glanced at Carla, widened her eyes and shook her head briefly. To her, it sounded like Gail was still lying. But why? "Look at me, Gail."

Gail's head pulled up sluggishly, and her gaze met Sara's. "No, nothing, I swear. The trust, it was gone. I found myself checking his phone several times a day, to see if he'd had any contact with her. I hated what we'd become. Living our lives on the edge. It was stressful at times. I had to walk around here with a mask on my face, keeping my unhappiness hidden from the children."

One word in that statement struck a chord with Sara... Mask! *Is she one of the killers? Is there more to this woman than meets the eye?*

"Did you try visiting a counsellor together?"

"Nope, he refused to go."

"Forgive me for asking this, but I need to know. Was this the first time your husband had strayed, to your knowledge?"

Gail remained tight-lipped for a while and then shook her head slowly. "No, he's had a number of affairs since we got wed. I've spent most of my marriage forgiving him for one affair or another."

Jesus! What a bloody revelation! What the fuck am I supposed to do with that information now? "The whole twenty years? Who else knew about his affairs?"

"His sister, Emma."

Sara felt duped by the pair of them. Sickened by their deception. Why? Why had they done it? Anger seared her veins. Betrayal and deception, two of her most hated vices, and here she was having to deal with both of them. How could she trust either of them again? Who knew what other secrets they were keeping from her? Sara rose from her chair. "I'm sorry, I know how this probably looks to you, but you're going to have to forgive me. If I don't leave now, I'm liable to explode. Both you and Emma are guilty of trying to derail this investigation, and the more I learn of your deception, the more likely I am not to believe a word that comes out of your mouths. I hope when we're gone, you take a long hard look at yourself and regret your actions. If you don't, then there's no point in me talking to you in the future. Maybe you and Emma are in cahoots with each other, is that it? We know there were two intruders that night, both wearing masks. Who's to say they weren't you and Emma, eh?"

"You have no right coming into my house and accusing me of killing him after what that man put me through over the years."

"Precisely, that's it in a nutshell, isn't it? You're the wronged woman, at the end of her tether, and you thought you'd end his life, right?"

"Get out of my house. I don't have to listen to this. I'm incensed that you should come here and accuse me of this when I'm in the process of grieving the man I love."

"Oh, come on! Give me some credit...the man you loved?"

"Okay, I think we should leave now," Carla said, pushing Sara gently towards the door.

Sara turned to glare at her partner, her blood boiling. Carla gave her a warning glare back.

"Okay, I'm done here. One last thing. I'll be contacting your insurance broker to make sure they don't pay out on your husband's life just yet. Not until I have fully completed my investigation."

"Get her out of here before I swing for her. As soon as you step outside that door, I'm going to put a call in to your superior. How dare you come here and speak to me like this?"

Sara stomped up the hallway, lost for words. She knew she'd gone too far and also knew she'd regret the day she let her tongue run away with her. She flung the front door open. It hit the wall and rebounded, clattering into Carla who was behind her.

"Gee, thanks," Carla muttered.

The door slammed shut after them. Carla stared at Sara and opened her mouth to speak.

Sara cut her off. "Leave it until we're in the car."

They slipped into the car and left the drive. Sara pulled up in a lay-by close to the house and switched off the engine. Her head hit the steering wheel, and she bounced in place a few times, the pain dulling the anger considerably with each strike.

"Fucking hell, Sara! Did you have to do that?"

She turned to face Carla. "I can't abide being lied to. Everything I said back there was the truth. Between them all, they've made a laughing stock out of us. How dare they tell us lie after sodding lie?"

"They've hardly done that. You need to keep that temper of yours under control, Sara, or the chief is going to come down heavy on you."

"I'll have a word with her when I get back to base. Shit! She bloody wound me up."

"That much is evident. Jesus, he was the one in the wrong, *not* her."

"Don't lecture me, Carla. I know I overstepped the mark."

Carla folded her arms and mumbled, "I think you should go back there and apologise to her."

"No way. I stand by what I said. She and Emma should have been honest with us from the outset." She fired up the engine and put her foot down. The tyres squealed as she floored the gas pedal.

"Hey, I'd like to get back to the station in one piece, if it's all the same to you."

"Sorry." Sara slowed to her normal speed and continued the journey in silence, her mind spinning after her uncharacteristic outburst.

They entered the station to find DCI Price standing at the top of the stairs, awaiting their arrival.

"Shit! She doesn't look happy," Sara grumbled as they ascended the stairs.

"DI Ramsey, in my office *now.*" The DCI marched back to her own office, expecting Sara to follow her.

Carla grabbed Sara's arm. "I hope it goes well for you."

"Thanks, partner."

Dread guided her steps into the office. DCI Price was holding the door open for her and slammed it shut once they were both inside.

"Ma'am, I can explain."

"Save it. Sit down."

Sara sat opposite DCI Price's large comfortable chair and waited for the chief to join her. Instead, Carol Price patrolled the floor behind her while she said what she had to say. "I'm appalled. Absolutely flabbergasted to receive a call from a victim's wife, slating my lead investigator. What were you thinking? Shut up, don't answer that, it was rhetorical. In fact, don't speak until I've finished laying into you. Because that's what I'm about to do. You've brought shame on this station with your outburst."

"But, ma'am, I can exp—"

"I told you not to interrupt me. If I have to shove some tape on your mouth, I will, don't tempt me. As I was saying…how dare you go round there and be so unprofessional? The poor woman was beside herself when she rang me. I thought you were settled now, taking life easier, had chilled out considerably compared to when you first showed up. I guess I was wrong. What possessed you to shout at the woman? Go on, you can speak now."

"Thank you. She lied to us. She and her sister-in-law have both lied, continued to lie, since Alistair Daly's death. How am I supposed to react to that sort of thing?"

"By not having a fucking showdown with a grieving widow would be a bloody start. Jesus, what about being tactful for a change?"

Sara turned in her seat to face Price. "I slipped up. I admit it. There's no need to keep shoving it down my throat, boss."

"You're in my office. If I want to keep reminding you of your shortcomings, I'll do it. Got that?"

"Yes, boss. Sorry."

"If you're admitting you're in the wrong, tell me this, when did you realise your mistake?"

"Not long after we left her house."

"Fucking hell. Why didn't you turn back and apologise to the poor woman? Why let it come to her ringing up to make a formal complaint about you? Because, I'm telling you, that's what this amounts to."

"Shit! Carla said the same thing in the car."

"Ugh…are you telling me that when your partner offers sound advice, you choose to ignore her? May I ask why? Is it that damned pride of yours getting in the way again?"

"No, it's nothing of the sort. I'm sorry, I can't keep apologising. What's done is done." Sara lowered her head in shame, her stomach tying itself into knots.

"Of all the people serving under me, you're the one person I never thought I'd have to read the riot act to. Bloody hell, what were you thinking? I can't ignore something like this. I'm gobsmacked and absolutely horrified by your behaviour. There's no way I can sweep this under the carpet." The more the chief spoke, the more her voice rose. "You know what this could mean, don't you? No? Right, let me tell you: the end of your *fucking* career, at least as you know it. The question is, do I have it in me to fight tooth and nail to keep you as a DI? And you know what, I'm seriously unsure whether I know the answer. Why should I defend such actions?"

"Because of my past record."

"And only because of that. Why do it? Why go round there and have a go at the woman?"

Sara sighed heavily. "I can't abide being lied to."

"Then I need you to reassess whether you want to continue serving in the force because a majority of our job is handling liars. Are you telling me you're unlikely to be able to do that role in the future?"

"No," she mumbled, aware of how true the chief's words were.

"Then what? How, if I can persuade the Super to overlook this complaint, are you going to go about doing your job in the future? By melting down every time someone you're dealing with tells you a lie?

Because that's the impression I'm getting from all of this. Jesus, what in God's name were you thinking, enlighten me?"

"If you'll allow me to speak without shouting at me, I'll try and tell you."

DCI Price finally sat in her chair. She glared at Sara and crossed her arms, her chest rising and falling heavily, indicating how angry she was, in case Sara hadn't picked up on it in her tone.

"It's an important case. One that has already led to two further people being tortured. One of those people is now lying in the mortuary fridge. I think I had every right having a go at Mrs Daly. If she and her sister-in-law had told me the truth from the beginning, maybe those other two people wouldn't have been subjected to the heinous crimes."

DCI Price ran a hand across her face. When she spoke, her voice had softened considerably. "I wasn't aware of the other two victims. That doesn't make what you did right, though, Sara. Although I can understand why you would be upset."

"Upset? I'm not upset, I'm bloody furious. You know how important the first days of an investigation are. To be lied to by everyone we spoke to…well, it infuriated me beyond words. Why would his family do that? You can't tell me I'm in the wrong, boss. She had it coming to her. How do we know that the family aren't in this together?"

"Ah, yes, that's another thing Mrs Daly mentioned. Why the fuck would you tell her that? Even if that's what you believe professionally, experience should tell you not to bloody say anything to the frigging woman."

Sara raised her arms out to the side and dropped them again. "My anger took over, and I could do nothing to prevent it. Two people are dead, and one is sitting in the hospital with life-changing wounds. How do you expect me to react when the family is covering something up?"

"I expect you to represent this force professionally at all times while you're on duty. Is that understood?"

"Yes, ma'am. Again, I regret my actions. If you want me to resign, then so be it." She searched her jacket pocket, extracted her warrant card and slammed it on the desk.

"Don't be ridiculous. Now you're just being childish."

"Am I? All I'm guilty of is speaking up for the victims, surely you can see that?"

DCI Price glanced out of her office window for a few seconds. She turned back to Sara and nodded. "I must have a screw loose, but yes, I believe you. I just hope the Super doesn't call for my resignation as well as yours, once I've had a chat with him."

"Damn. I regret putting you in this position, it wasn't my intention. I never meant for any of this to happen."

"I have always trusted you, I'm not about to stop doing that, and I have no intention of throwing you into the lions' den. My suggestion would be not to contact Mrs Daly again. Will you be able to objectively continue with this investigation?"

"I believe I'll be able to do that, boss. I'm desperate to bring these bastards to justice."

"Then go. Leave me to clear up the shit you've created." DCI Price pointed at her. "I don't want to see you in my office again under such circumstances in the future, am I making myself clear?"

Sara stood. "Yes, boss. Thank you." She left the office on heavy legs and took a moment to gather her thoughts in the corridor before she went back to the incident room.

Carla looked her way as soon as she entered. Sara winked at her, letting her know everything was all right and that she hadn't had any body parts torn off by the chief.

She spent the rest of the afternoon with her heart not in the case, buried in her office doing paperwork. Carla entered the room with a caffeine fix at around four.

"Are you locking yourself away on purpose?"

Sara kept her head bowed, knowing that if their gazes locked Carla would see the truth.

"Come on...what is it you're always touting, don't kid a kidder?"

She glanced up. "Sometimes you're too smart for your own good. I'm fine. Just leave me to my own pity party for a few more hours until it's home time."

Carla flopped into the spare chair and tutted. "And then what?"

"I go home and hit a nice bottle of red I've had my eye on for a few months which was a present from Mark."

"Ha! And do you think that's going to solve your problems, seeing them at the bottom of a glass?"

"No, not at all, and I can do without you scolding me as if I were a teenager."

"There's an obvious answer to that...stop behaving like one then."

Sara narrowed her eyes. She was doing no such thing, was she? "Was there a point to your visit, Sergeant?"

"I was going to bring you up to speed on what we've discovered, except I can tell you're not interested."

"Cut the crap and spill."

"Got ya! So you are still interested in the case, despite giving the impression that you're not."

"Piss off, Carla, once a copper always a copper, of course I'm still interested in the damn case. Even though the first victim's wife has reported me."

Carla shrugged and eye-rolled her. "And you're shocked by that?"

"No. I'm disconcerted by it, if you must know. Go on, what have you stumbled across?"

"Er...nothing. We've tried our hardest to track down Elizabeth Atley, but she appears to have vanished."

"Could she have moved to a different area? We can't really pin this on her yet, not until we're certain of her whereabouts."

"I thought about that. My idea is that if her intention is not to be found, then that definitely puts her in the frame for this, right?"

"Maybe. Who knows? It's pure conjecture on your part at present. For all we know she could have gone abroad and started up somewhere else once the affair ended. When did the landlord say she did a moonlight flit?"

"A couple of months ago."

"And no one has either seen or heard from her since then? Sounds suspicious to me. What about her parents, have you tried tracing them?"

"Will's on it now. He rang Emma earlier to try and see if she had their address on the personnel file."

"And?"

"Emma wasn't there. Someone at the firm said she'd gone home early with a headache and had no intention of going back there today."

"I bet that's guilt rearing its head."

Carla groaned. "Let it go, Sara, you're better than this."

Sara picked up a pen and jabbed the point on the paper in front of her. "I know I am. I hate being this bitter, it's no picnic for me, you know. But what I hate even more is the fact that I've been lied to. It's as if his wife and his sister have colluded to keep us in the dark. Whether that was intentional on their part or not, I despise that it's happened."

"I get that. Look, if you don't get past this issue you have with them, well, we might as well give the investigation up. In other words, it's going to eat away at you and make you seriously ill. Your impartiality is going to be cloudy, which in turn could put more people's lives at risk."

Sara dropped the pen, folded her arms and leaned back. "So what are you suggesting we do then?"

"Start chasing the pathologist, see what she has to offer in the form of DNA. That has to be our initial go-to card, doesn't it? Without that evidence, we'll be struggling to pin anything on this Atley woman. At the moment, all she's guilty of, in my eyes anyway, is having an affair with a victim."

Sara sighed and chewed the inside of her mouth as she contemplated her partner's suggestion. "Okay. I'll make the call now and suffer Lorraine's wrath for chasing her too early for the results."

"Then so be it. It's better than sitting here twiddling our damn thumbs, right?"

"Smarty pants. Okay, leave me to it."

Carla stood to leave.

"Thanks for the much-needed kick up the arse."

"Always a pleasure. You're an excellent copper, Sara. You're foolish to let people's idiotic attitudes steer you off course. There, I've said my piece now. Let me know what Lorraine has to say...umm... you'll probably need to paraphrase it without the expletives, knowing her."

They both chuckled, and Sara felt a little more human after her partner's wise words. She dialled the mortuary's number and waited to be patched through to Lorraine who answered her call as brusque as ever.

"If you're ringing up to see what results I've got for you then you're wasting not only your time, but mine, as well."

"Hello to you, too. It was a courtesy call really, to bring you up to speed on things at this end."

"Go on then. I haven't got all day, mate."

"The first male victim was having an affair, and I have a stomach-clenching gut instinct that the woman involved is our killer."

"Whoa! Just because they were having an affair?"

"Not only that, she used to work at the builders' yard with him, and he sacked her."

"Okay, that's more like it, however, I still think you're guilty of overthinking things. Trying to squeeze a square peg into a round hole."

"Call me stupid, if you like, but if you'd let me finish, there's also a third issue that I'd like to factor into my logic."

"Pardon me for shooting down your ideas when you're on a roll. Go on, pray tell?"

Sara pulled a face at the phone. "This woman is missing."

"I see. You've got me on that one. Hang on...what if she's gone missing because she's *dead*?"

"Where the hell did that come from?"

"What if Daly bumped her off, and someone found out about it and got their revenge on her behalf?"

"Someone, as in a family member?"

"How the fuck should I know? I was simply throwing it out there for you to consider. Come on, Sara, what's going on?" Her obtuse tone gave way to a far gentler one.

"I lost it with the wife, and she complained about me."

"You did what? Wait, I need to sit down to hear this doozy."

She could always count on Lorraine to lend a sympathetic ear, not.

"You know how much I detest liars. I let rip and gave her what for. She lied, end of. She, and Emma, come to that, should've told me Alistair was having an affair. All we ask is that people respect our integrity and offer us the clues to try to solve a case."

"Granted. I'll give you that one. And yes, I agree and would've also been livid, except I would have restrained myself. She's grieving, for fuck's sake."

"I'm aware of that. Thank you, as always, for pointing out my imperfections, it's duly noted."

"Shut up. I'm here for you, ring me anytime and sound off, just don't bloody take it out on the family members."

"Yeah, I had that same conversation with the DCI earlier this afternoon."

"Jesus. I'm surprised you're still at work. You are, aren't you?"

"I am, by the skin of my teeth. I've ballsed up big time, and there's nowt I can do about it."

"Bollocks. You can stop wallowing, get off your frigging fat arse—that was a joke by the way—and do something about it. Preferably go out there and hunt down the killer or killers."

"There are two of them, or so we believe. I had a brief chat with Jeanette when she came around from the anaesthetic. She told me there were two intruders wearing masks."

"And you still think this woman has something to do with these heinous crimes?"

"Wearing a mask...which could be one way for her to cover up her true identity and gender."

"Hmm...okay, I can see where you're coming from. Right, I'm going to have to love you and leave you. I'm just about to start the PM on Bob Lockett, and no, I haven't got any DNA results for you yet. Goodbye, I hope your day improves."

"Thanks, Lorraine. Ring me as soon as you get the results."

"Don't I always?"

"That's debatable. Speak soon." She ended the call, unsure whether she felt more positive now she'd spoken to her friend or not.

6

"She's early."

"We can't go in there yet, it's broad daylight still. We'd better leave it a few hours."

They had arrived at the house on a stakeout, to check what the lay of the land was regarding the neighbours et cetera. The last thing they'd anticipated was Emma coming home early.

"What if she's expecting someone?"

Micky Quaker narrowed his eyes and watched their next target let herself into the detached house. "So what? The more the merrier as far as I'm concerned."

"I can't keep doing this. It seems to me like you're enjoying it far more than you should do."

"And? What's your damn point?"

"I didn't want things to go this far."

He turned to look at her. "You're not backing out on me, are you?"

"What if I was?"

"You'd make me angry. You know what happens when I'm fuelled with anger." He laughed.

"Is this necessary? Don't you think she, or they, have suffered enough now?"

"Do you? After what they did to you?"

"Sometimes I think yes, and other times I think they deserve a whole lot more."

"Then we stick to our plan and tick people off the list."

She sat there, staring at the house, regretting her decision to get involved with Micky in the first place. When they'd started dating, she got the impression he was a decent bloke. He had romanced her into his bed, and that was where the spark of an idea had been formulated. Unfortunately, after the first murder, that was when she'd found out what drove him. He'd revealed that night, during their sex session, what type of thrill he got from torturing people. Even more so, when they'd done the dirty on her. He'd professed his love for her. Now, well now, she just felt trapped in a world so alien to her that it scared her. He'd also revealed during one of their romps between the sheets, that he'd served time for GBH a few years prior to them getting together.

Elizabeth spent most of her days pacifying him, unsure what he was likely to do to her if she ever pissed him off. A nasty glint had appeared in his eye once he'd begun torturing Alistair, and it had dawned on her then that she was in too deep and they were on an express train to self-destruction. He was unhinged, and she could see no way of escaping the hold he had on her. He'd thrashed her after he'd killed Bob Lockett, because she'd objected to his death. They had gone there to teach him and his wife a lesson, not to end his ruddy life.

All she wanted to do was leave this moron, but she had no money to her name. He'd stripped her of the payoff Alistair had given her, her final salary. He'd spent that eons ago on booze and fags. *Her* money. And now she had nothing to help her obtain a way out.

"You're quiet, what's up? You having second thoughts?"

Second, third and fourth thoughts actually, but I'm not about to share that with you.

He grasped her hand, settled down in his seat, rested his head against the window and promptly fell asleep. Why had she got involved with him, with anyone after Alistair had ended it? Why didn't she take the money and go somewhere else? Why had she fallen under Micky's spell when all she wanted was to be with Alistair? *I'm such a hypocrite. I allowed him to torture Alistair and to eventually kill him. Why did I do that if I still truly loved him?*

The more she mulled things over, the more confused she got about her feelings and her motive to continue to be with this man. She was stuck with him, for now. Even when he was asleep, he clung to her, ensuring that she couldn't get away from him. *Does he know how much I want to break free from him? He must do, otherwise he'd trust me to be out of his sight for a few moments.* Even when she visited the loo, he was there, waiting at the door for her to come out. She was too involved to try to do anything about it. And if she considered giving him a false address for the next victim, well, she was pretty certain she knew what that would lead to.

Stuck! That's what she was. No, worse than that, trapped. In a love-less relationship with a man who took great pleasure in seeking revenge on those who had wronged her. *How fucking warped is that?*

She let herself drift off to sleep rather than sit there staring at the house for the next few hours as they waited for dusk to descend. He shook her arm and planted a slobbery wet kiss on her lips to wake her. She stretched, thinking she was waking from a restful night's sleep in her semi-comfortable bed.

"Hello, my Sleeping Beauty. Have I told you lately how much I love you?"

"Yes, all the time."

He grabbed her around the throat. "Uh-uh! Wrong answer. You're supposed to respond by telling me how much you love me back."

She tried to wriggle out of his hand. "I'm sorry, please forgive me. You woke me up, and I was disorientated there for a moment or two."

"So, say it!"

"I love you with all my heart, Micky." *I hope I don't choke on the lie. The sooner I'm rid of this jerk the better. I can then go on and live my life the way I want to...without fear.*

He kissed her full on the lips, pulled away and studied every inch of her face. "God was really looking down on me when you walked into my life, darling."

Strange, I think the Devil was looking down on me when you walked into mine. C'est la vie!

She issued a sugary-sweet smile. "I think the same, sweetheart. You're wonderful to me. Take care of me the way no other man has done in the past. For that, I'll be eternally grateful to you."

"Glad to hear it." His attention returned to what was going on outside the vehicle. "Right, it's getting darker now. Another half an hour should do it. We'll make our move then. Did you bring the sandwiches?"

"Yes, I put them in the boot with the holdalls."

"I'll get them. You stay in the warm."

He left the door open and hopped out of the car. He was back within a few seconds. Even if the thought had crossed her mind about escaping, she wouldn't have had the time to have fulfilled her aim. *Trapped.*

They sat and ate their cheese and pickle sandwiches on white bread, the only type he insisted having at the flat, as if they were on a trip out in the country having a delicious picnic. How she managed to swallow her sandwich past the lump embedded in her throat, she'd never know. As her sandwich travelled down her oesophagus, she had to say a silent prayer for it not to resurface. *How can he think about eating at a time like this? I can tell what's passing through his mind right now. The pain he's about to inflict on Emma, judging by the grin on his face.*

"Eat up. I've finished mine," he said, eyeing up the rest of hers.

She handed her half-eaten sandwich to him. Seconds later, he'd scoffed the lot and swilled it down with a can of Coke, followed by a deafening belch that made her cringe. *Jesus wept, whatever did I see in him?*

"Ready?"

She nodded. "Let's do this," she replied, keeping up the bravado for his benefit and ignoring her true feelings.

"What are we waiting for? Get your mask on and let the show begin."

She followed him out of the car, picked up one of the holdalls in the boot and marched with him across the road to Emma's house. He rang the bell. They donned their masks and spun around once they heard the door open. Emma was quick—she tried to push the door closed again, but Micky stuck his foot in the gap and yelped out when the pain jolted up his leg.

"You bitch, I'm going to make you pay for that."

Emma screamed. Micky gave her an uppercut to the chin. He'd told Elizabeth one of his greatest heroes was Mike Tyson. Why hadn't that surprised her? Once she'd found out that snippet of information, perhaps she should have turned and run. *What's done is done, I'd better get used to it.*

Emma stumbled backwards, her head smashing into the hall mirror hanging on the wall. Elizabeth closed the front door swiftly behind her in case Emma tried screaming again to alert the neighbours.

Micky latched on to Emma's hair and yanked her through the house. Emma's arms were flailing, trying desperately to swipe at him. Elizabeth's heart tugged when it shouldn't have, not after what she'd been guilty of in the past.

The three of them were in the kitchen now at the back of the house. It was warm; the radiators were on full blast.

Micky was quick to notice this and snarled in Emma's face, "Do you need it this hot, bitch? Ever thought of conserving some energy? Nah, I didn't think so. Tie her up."

He held Emma at arm's length, allowing Elizabeth to wrap the rope around Emma several times. He then shoved her into a chair. They hadn't discussed what type of torture he would be using on her, so Elizabeth gasped when he withdrew a mini blowtorch, the type chefs use. He glanced her way and glared at her, his eyes dark with intent peering through the peepholes in his mask. She dropped her head in shame. Might even have said a silent prayer to help Emma, not that she'd ever divulge that to him, once this was over.

All this was going on behind Emma's back. She tried to peer over her shoulder and met his fist again. "Please, don't hurt me. I know I'm probably wasting my time pleading with you after what you did to my brother. Please, won't you tell me what this is all about? Who are you? Why are you doing this?"

"What does it matter?" Micky snarled close to her face.

"It would help me make sense of it all."

He laughed and tipped back his head. "And where would the fun be in that?"

Emma faced Elizabeth. "Don't let him do this to me, please?"

Elizabeth shook her head, surprised her eyes moistened with tears. *What am I doing here? Why do this to her? To them? What have I got myself into? And where the fuck is it all going to end? With my death? Is that what he has planned?*

Micky got out his lighter and lit the blowtorch. At first, he toyed with it, getting it close to different parts of Emma's body. "You like the heat, don't you? You're going to enjoy this even more, I assure you. You'd better get the tape out of the bag. She's gonna scream the house down otherwise once I get started peeling her flesh."

Elizabeth resisted the temptation to shudder. The thought of what Emma was about to be subjected to appalled her. If there was any way she could prevent him having his fun she would jump in and help Emma. The trouble was, she was at a loss to know what to do for the best. Once his mind was set on something, there was no changing it. That much had been beaten into her over the past few months.

He paid attention to Emma's right arm. The blowtorch inched its way closer to her skin. Elizabeth took the opportunity to glance around. Sitting on the worktop, barely a foot away from her, was a six-piece knife set in a knife block. She presumed the ones in the back row were the larger blades. *If only I had the balls to reach for one while he's distracted. What good would it do me? He'd turn on me in a flash and wouldn't think twice about using the blowtorch on me. Shit! Shit! And triple shit!*

The tape did the trick of suppressing Emma's screams as the immediate air took on the smell of singed flesh, Emma's flesh.

Micky roared with laughter. A crazed laugh which terrified the crap out of her. *How can he do this to a woman? This is far worse than the others had suffered. Why? Is there something deep in his past he hasn't disclosed to me yet?*

He took a breather and walked a couple of feet to stand in front of

Emma. He lowered his head to within a few inches of hers, the devilment in his eyes evident behind the mask. Elizabeth had to fight hard to keep her sandwich down.

"Do you want to feel yet more heat, Emma?"

Emma sniffled and shook her head. The tape muffled any likely response, not that Micky would give a toss.

"Here we go. I bet you use factor fifty sitting on the beach in the Med, don't you? Protecting that pretty face of yours. Well, we'll see about that, see how hot you really like it." He poised the torch close to her face and glanced up at Elizabeth. "No, I have a better idea, *you* do it."

Before Elizabeth was fully aware of what he was up to, he ripped her mask off. The look on Emma's face was one of shock and even horror. Her eyes widened, and her inaudible pleas filled the room again.

"No, I can't," Elizabeth said, taking a step backwards.

Micky beckoned her with a curling finger.

She retreated another few paces. "I can't, not to her."

Emma closed her eyes.

"You'll do as I say…or suffer the consequences, bitch."

Why the switch? Why was he speaking to her like that? Where was the love he'd bestowed upon her in the car, not ten minutes earlier?

She shook her head and backed up into the counter. Her brain worked its magic, figured out quickly that she was within spitting distance of the knives. *What if I reach for one? He's quicker than me. I couldn't stand it if he turned the torch on me. I'm in a catch-twenty-two position. Damned if I do and damned if I don't. Please, don't make me do this.*

Terrified, and scared of what he'd do to her if she repeatedly said no, she took the torch from his hand.

"That's it, come on now, baby, it'll be fun. Revenge, remember, that's why we're here." He walked towards her, his gaze zeroed in on hers, and guided her hand to within inches of Emma's face. Elizabeth closed her eyes, determined not to see the mutilation she was about to inflict.

"Open them," he demanded, his head close to hers. He removed his mask, revealing the pure hatred etched into his features. There was no turning back now, that much was apparent. His hand pushed hers.

As much as she wanted to drop the torch, or better still, turn it on him, the scowl across his features warned her what would happen if she did.

"We haven't got all day. Actually, we have, but we need to get out of here. I have something else up my sleeve."

She faced him and frowned. "What? I need to know."

"All you need is to finish this bitch off before I turn the tables on you, got that?"

She nodded. Her aim had been to waste time in delaying Emma's torture. Now her time had run out, she had two people's fates in her hand, Emma's and her own. After considering why they were here for a few seconds, she realised there was only one way out of this situation. To do as they'd intended, to torture and kill Emma, and if she didn't…that didn't bear thinking about.

She squinted as the torch closed in on Emma's face. Emma squealed behind the tape, and then nothing. Elizabeth's eyes flew open. What the hell was going on? She couldn't be dead, could she?

He stood in front of her, and after checking Emma's pulse, he laughed. "She's fainted. I'm going to bring her around. Take a breather while I do that."

Elizabeth put the torch down on the worktop beside her and inched backwards. While he was distracted trying to revive Emma, she reached behind her and slipped a large knife from the block and hid it up the sleeve of her bomber jacket, hoping the elasticated edge would prevent the knife from dropping out.

Emma was coming to. "Wakey, wakey, bitch. Did you miss us? We missed you. Now, where were we…ah yes, Elizabeth, you were about to exact your revenge. Feel free to pick up where you left off. I'm enjoying the entertainment and keeping my hands clean for a change. Maybe I'll leave all this torturing lark to you from now on. Nah, I'd soon get bored, not having the control at my fingertips. It's empowering once you get over your first-time nerves, I assure you."

"I don't mind you having the control, I'll watch."

He shook his head slowly. "You're not getting out of it that easy. Now, get on with it, we have to be somewhere else soon."

"Where?" she queried.

"You'll find out soon enough…after we've dealt with her. I won't tell you again, get on with it," he sneered.

Elizabeth moved forward a couple of inches, her gaze locked on to Emma's. "This is your fault, and Alistair's, of course. Once you found out we were having an affair, you were evil to me. Don't look at me like that, as if I'm the one in the wrong." Where she dug up the courage to point the torch at Emma's skin she'd never know. The smell of burning flesh made her retch. She watched the terror emanate from Emma in droves, then there was nothing.

Micky checked Emma over and shook his head. "You've killed her. Maybe we'll think twice about using the torch on the next one. I hate it when things don't go according to plan and the torture is over in a flash." He laughed and removed the torch from her grip, switched the flame off and set it on the worktop to cool down for a moment. "What do you propose doing now?"

He wiggled his eyebrows, and her stomach clenched at the thought of having sex with him.

"Shouldn't we get out of here? What if someone rings the bell?"

"Who's likely to do that then?"

"I don't know. I'm scared. All I want to do is get as far away from here as possible. Save what you have in mind for when we get home."

He touched the torch and kept his hand on it for a few seconds. "Okay, you've got your wish. This is cold enough to put away now. Let's go."

He packed the bag, grabbed her hand, and together they fled the house.

She left the front door ajar, hoping someone would find Emma soon. She despised herself. There was no way she couldn't, after seeing the woman suffer excruciating pain. She had to put an end to this, but how? Things had already got way out of hand, gone further than she'd ever intended. For what…revenge? Was it truly worth it?

7

*T*he morning was cold and damp. Sara and Carla met up in the car park and entered the station together. One look at the desk sergeant's face, and Sara realised something was badly amiss.

"Morning, Jeff, what's wrong?" Sara asked, concerned.

"I wouldn't bother going upstairs if I were you, ma'am, you're needed at a crime scene."

Sara ran a hand through her hair and heaved out a sigh. "Not another one. Do we know who the victim is this time?"

He nodded. Something in the way he was staring at her told her she wasn't going to like his answer. "Emma Daly."

"What? No way! This can't be bloody happening. Come on, Carla, let's go. The crime scene, is it at her home?" she flung over her shoulder as she opened the door again.

"Yes, boss. I'll ring my guys at the scene, make them aware that you'll be attending."

"Thanks. Tell my team as well, Jeff, if you would?" She raced to her vehicle. "Get in, we'll take my car. What the fuck? Shit! I told her to stay elsewhere. Why don't people frigging listen to me?"

"Calm down. We don't know the ins and outs of what's gone on yet, not until we get there."

"I have a pretty good idea. She'll have been tortured like the others...shit! Are we prepared for this? For what we're about to encounter?" Sara drove to Emma's address under the blues and twos and screeched to a halt alongside a patrol car around seven minutes later. Not bad going, considering the state of the roads.

She and Carla slipped on their white suits and entered the house.

Lorraine and her team were already there, doing the necessary. "Ah, there you are. This is about as gruesome as it gets, ladies, so prepare yourselves."

Sara accepted her guidance and peered around Lorraine at the victim, at Emma. "Bloody hell! What in God's name possesses someone to do that to another person? Was it a lighter?"

"Despicable, right? No, I've seen something similar to this a few years back. My take is the perp used one of those blowtorches, you know, the mini ones, the type the chefs use."

"Jesus. That's way up there in the sick mind realm, isn't it? The poor woman, she didn't deserve to go out like that."

"Let's face it, who does? That's my guesstimate at this time. I'll know more once I get her on the table at the mortuary."

Sara fell silent, her thoughts with the rest of the family. "Shit! What about the others? They're going to need some form of protection now. The killers obviously have an agenda and are working their way through the family. I warned Emma to find somewhere to stay but didn't warn the others."

Carla pointed a finger in the air. "Maybe not only the family, just the people who worked for the builders' merchants. Don't forget the assistant manager and his wife in this scenario."

Sara chewed her lip and nodded. "You're right. Why? If it is this Elizabeth, she's one sad lady if she's going around killing people just because she was sacked."

Lorraine nodded. "There is that. I need to get on, ladies, if you don't mind. I've received another call telling me there's been a fatal crash on the A4103 between here and the Hop Pocket. Joy of joys, when you're the only pathologist covering the area because of dumb cuts."

Sara flinched. "I thought you were about to say something else then."

Lorraine inclined her head. "Oh right, you thought I was going to insert an 'n' into the word *cuts*. Yeah, that would work as well. Excuse me."

Sara and Carla stepped away from the victim. Sara shook her head over and over.

Carla tugged on her arm and wagged a finger at her. "I recognise that look. Don't you dare feel guilty about this."

Sara threw her hands up in the air. "How else am I going to feel? We need to concentrate all our efforts on finding that Atley woman before she does yet more damage."

"All right, but first you need to take a few deep breaths and calm down."

"I am calm. Actually, you're right. I need to get out of here, the smell is driving me crazy."

They stepped outside the house again and gulped down lungfuls of fresh air. Sara was beside herself, riddled with guilt for not protecting the other members of the family and the assistant manager before Emma.

"Where is it all going to end? What could her motive be? Hear me out here, I can understand if she's a wronged woman going after Alistair, but Bob and Emma? Where's the logic in that?"

"We won't know the answer to that puzzle until we find her. We can't do that standing around here."

"There's nothing we can do if she's bloody disappeared off the face of the earth," Sara retorted, exasperated.

"You're not thinking straight. There's plenty we can do. I'll ring the station, see if the team can cobble together the CCTV footage for the roads close to here. She must've got here by car or some other form of transport. There was nothing showing up under her old address for a vehicle."

"Her accomplice, there's two of them, remember? He or she must be using their vehicle to get around the various crime scenes."

"Then we need to track it down. It's the only possible lead we've got so far."

"Lead? Can you call it that when we have nothing yet?"

"You're right, my bad to refer to it as that." Carla removed her phone from her pocket and rang the station. "Ah, Barry, just the man I want to speak to," she said, putting the phone on speaker. "You're aware that we're at another crime scene and the location. We need you to search through the CCTV for us, see if you can pick up a car carrying this Elizabeth Atley."

"Wow, okay, I'll see what I can do. How many people do you want assigned to this task?"

"As many as possible," Carla said, glancing up at Sara for her approval.

Sara nodded and sighed.

"Roger that. Is it as bad as the desk sergeant said it was?"

"Worse. Not pretty. We're going to stick around here doing house-to-house. We'll hopefully be back in a few hours. Ring us if you stumble across anything in the meantime."

"Will do."

Carla ended the call.

"Which side do you want?" Sara asked.

"I'll go left and you go right. Want to whizz through them?"

"We'll take as long as necessary, Carla."

"Consider me told. I'm off."

Sara collected her thoughts and got back to the job at hand—asking yet another round of mind-numbing questions which had so far proven to be pointless at the previous scene. She knocked on the first door, the house directly next to Emma's. A woman with long blonde hair and striking makeup opened it.

Sara flashed her warrant card. "DI Sara Ramsey. Mind if I come in and have a quick word with you?"

"Yes, I do mind. I'm on my way to work. I have an important meeting to attend this morning, if it's all the same to you."

"It won't take a minute. We're conducting a murder inquiry."

That made the woman rethink her offhand attitude. She gasped and covered her mouth with her shaking hand. "No, not Emma?"

"Yes, I'm afraid so. All right if I come in?" she asked again, already chilled to the bone with the wind whirling in the street behind her.

"Sorry, yes. Come in."

Sara closed the front door and followed the woman into a grand lounge. It was immaculately presented, not a cushion or throw out of place. A row of silver photo frames, displaying either friends or family, sat proudly on the mantelpiece, the focal point of the room.

"Take a seat. I'm in shock. How can this happen? This is usually a quiet, respectable neighbourhood. A wonderful place to live, so much so that houses rarely come onto the market, unless there's been a death in the family. Oh, gosh, I'm sorry to waffle, I'm in... Emma was really friendly and went out of her way to say hello every day, either going to work or on the way home."

"I've met her a few times over the last couple of days and found her to be very pleasant. Can I ask if you were at home last night?"

"No, I was out with my husband. We were at a friend's birthday party."

"Was that local?"

"Yes, we had a table booked in town, at Miller and Carter."

"Ah yes, I know the one. What time did you leave and return home?"

She tilted her head as she thought. "The leaving part I can give a definite answer to, it's the coming home I'm struggling with."

"Roughly will do."

"We left just after seven-fifteen. A taxi collected us. I suppose we came home between eleven and eleven-ten."

Sara jotted down the times in her notebook. "Did you happen to see anything out of the ordinary when you returned?"

"Such as? Someone hanging around outside Emma's?"

"Either that, or a strange car parked up outside her house, or at the end of the road perhaps?"

She shook her head slowly. "No, I don't think so. Not that I can remember. I wasn't really looking out for anyone, though. Sorry."

"That's fine. Don't worry. We believe whoever did this were professionals anyway."

"Hitmen of sorts?"

"Not quite. People with a vendetta, let's leave it at that."

"But why Emma, why her?"

"Are you aware that her brother lost his life a few days ago?"

"No…" The word gushed out of her attached to a large breath.

"I'm afraid so."

"Both of them were killed by the same person, is that what you're saying?"

"We're looking into that at present. First impressions would indicate that to be the case. One final question before I leave. Have you noticed anyone possibly hanging around in the last week or so?"

"No, I'm sorry, I really wish I could help you. I'm the least observant person I know."

"It doesn't matter, it was a long shot. Thank you for your time. All right if I leave you a card?"

"I was just about to ask for one. I'll have a chat with Dave, my hubby, when he comes home and ring you if he can add anything."

"You're very kind. Thank you."

The woman showed her to the front door. "Sorry I couldn't be of more help to you. Hope you catch the person responsible. I'll be sure to up our security at the house, or get hubby to as soon as we can."

"I didn't get your name. Mrs?"

"Clarke, Joanna Clarke."

"I think that's wise, upping your security, you never know these days."

She nodded and closed the door. Sara hung around waiting for Carla to finish speaking to the man at the house on the opposite side of the road.

Carla spun around and flashed her a smile. "The chap called me over. He spotted a dark car parked a few doors down last night."

"Brilliant news. I don't suppose he got a look at the plate?"

"Part of it. He nipped to the loo and when he got back the car had gone."

"Never mind. We always have to do things the hard way. What time was this?"

"Around six-thirty. He saw the car out here for a while. Two people inside looked as if they were having a nap, or so he said."

"A nap? Can you believe that? Maybe they were staking the place out, waiting for Emma to come home."

"Not exactly. The woman at twenty-three told me that she saw Emma come home early yesterday, around three o'clock."

"Curiouser and curiouser."

"Want to hear what I think?"

"Go on," Sara replied, frowning.

"What if they were staking the place out until it got dark, then made their move?"

"Sounds feasible to me, smarty pants."

"Purely speculation on my part for now."

"Anything else?"

"Not yet. I'll ring Barry, tell him it's a dark car and give him the partial plate."

"You do that. I'll move on to the next one."

Sara crossed the road again and knocked on the second neighbour's door. An old man appeared in the doorway. "Hello, sir. I'm DI Sara Ramsey. All right if I step in and have a word with you for a few moments?"

"Not without some form of ID you're bloody not."

Sara grinned at him. "Nice to see you're on the ball, sir. I was testing you." She flashed her ID.

"Likely story, lass. Come in. Wipe your feet on the mat. The missus will have my guts for garters otherwise."

"I'd hate to be the cause of a domestic between you." She wiped her shoes thoroughly on the thick, wiry doormat.

"Come on, that'll do. Sharon's out at the moment, so no harm done. Just testing you," he said, returning her grin.

The man was a cheeky chappy who reminded Sara of her father.

The house was dated, full of furniture and knick-knacks going back to the seventies' era. Nothing modern, not even in the form of cushions on the sofa. Sara stood until the man instructed her to do otherwise.

"What are you waiting for? A number ten bus? Sit down, for goodness' sake."

"Thank you."

He leaned forward in his easy chair and whispered, "What's going on at that young lady's house then to warrant the police being here?"

"Miss Daly was attacked in her home last night."

"Never!" he replied, bouncing back in his seat.

"I'm afraid it's true, I would never jest about something as important as this."

"All right, duck. What can I do to help? Because I will if I have to. My brother used to walk the beat around this neck of the woods, back in the day. Poor sod popped his clogs a month ago. Cantankerous old shit, he'd become."

"I'm sorry to hear that. Did he serve long?"

"All his working life, well, until they pensioned him off, that is. Never been the same since, not really. He'd lost the will to live. He'd never married, you see, always touted that he was married to the job, damn idiot. He's had women flinging themselves at him from time to time, wasn't bloody interested in any of them. So he died a lonely old bastard. I bet his tadger was as shrivelled as the day he was born through lack of use over the years. Not what you wanted to hear, but hey ho."

Sara struggled to keep a straight face. "I haven't heard that word in years, thanks for brightening my day."

"What, tadger? And you're welcome. Now we've broken the ice, feel free to ask me anything you want, but we'll leave my sex life out of it, if you don't mind, that's between me and the missus."

Sara wasn't sure how she kept it together. She cleared her throat, forcing down the giggle that had settled there. "Anyway, the reason I'm here is to find out whether you can tell me anything about a car that was seen parked up yesterday by one of your neighbours."

"Are you having a laugh? I bet you're talking about old Albert, am I right?"

"I'm not sure on the man's name, sir. Which reminds me, what's yours?"

"Frankie Vaughan. Now don't go looking at me like that. My parents loved the singer. I've had a rough ride over the years from the mickey-takers, I can tell you."

"I bet. It actually suits you. Getting back to the car...?"

"Ah, yes. Old Albert, he sits there staring out of his window all day long—at least he must do because I always see him peering out behind that damn curtain of his."

"The car, as in, did you notice it?"

"Right, I'm with you. Nope, can't say I did. We're out the back here most of the day. Too noisy out the front; Sharon hates it. We switched the rooms around. We don't use a bloody dining room so it made sense. This one's a little bigger. Go on, another snippet of useless information you're not interested in, correct?"

"Sort of. Anyway, as I was saying, Emma Daly was attacked last night in her house, and we're making general enquiries to see if anyone either heard or saw anything untoward around here at the time of her attack."

"Bad, is she? Only I spotted the SOCO van. Is that a done thing these days, them showing up at a scene? Or is this something more than that?" He tapped the side of his nose. "I'm not stupid, love. I heard the commotion when all the vans turned up and saw people going in there in their suits. She's dead, ain't she?"

Sara shrugged. "She is, unfortunately. I kept that information from you in case it upset you."

"I can understand that. Bloody hell. A murder on our street. Well, that's an effing first."

She noticed the colour had drained from his cheeks. "Are you all right, Frankie?"

"I will be. Come as a bit of a shock, that has. Knocked the damn stuffing out of me to tell you the truth."

"I'm sorry. I had my doubts whether to share the news with you or not."

"It's all right. Don't you fret about me. Christ, I wish I had heard something. I would've tried to help that poor woman. I think we all would've, if we'd heard anything. Did any of the other neighbours hear anything?"

"We've only just started questioning people. Nothing has come to light so far."

"People aren't interested in what goes on in their community these days, are they?"

"Sometimes it's like that. It's difficult, I suppose everyone has their own busy life to lead."

"Aye, different to when I was a youngster starting out. Shame really, a lot goes unnoticed. Maybe that's why the crime rate is going up and up, eh?"

"Possibly. I think we lack the people walking the street, like your brother, keeping their eyes and ears open, nipping things in the bud long before they get a chance to escalate."

"Do you think we'll ever get those days back?"

"Highly unlikely. Anyway, the gentleman across the road is the only one to mention this car. At the moment, that's all we've got to go on. Do you get out and about much, Frankie?"

"Dodgy hip, duck, waiting for an op which is due in a few months. It means I've got limited mobility."

"Sorry to hear that. I hope the operation is a success and allows you to get around better. Over the past few days, have you seen or heard anyone talking about a stranger hanging around?"

"I wish I could say I had, but I haven't. Once the door is shut, Sharon and I are in our own little world. We haven't got any children, tend to while away the hours playing a game of cards out the back here."

Sara rose from her seat. "Never mind, it was worth a shot. Thanks for talking to me, Frankie. Take care of yourself."

"Good luck with your investigation. Do me a favour and pull the door to on your way out." He rubbed his left hip. "Bloody thing is playing up. Must be this damp weather."

"I'll do that. Nice meeting you." Sara left the house and moved on to the next one.

*a*n hour later, as Sara was stamping her feet in the numbing cold, checking they were still attached, Carla approached her. "How did you get on?"

"More about the car, nothing about the driver or passenger. Want me to see if Barry has found anything out yet?"

"I've had enough of wasting time around here. There are too many occupants to speak to. We've done our bit, questioning her immediate neighbours. We'll leave uniform to carry out the rest of the door-to-door enquiries. I could do with a coffee to warm up. Let's find a café."

"I'm not about to argue with that. Maybe a slice of cake will go down a treat as well."

"Come on, you cheeky mare. Isn't there a garden centre near here?"

"There is, just up the road."

They stopped off at the nursery a few minutes later, and Sara ordered a latte each and a huge slice of homemade chocolate cake.

While they waited to be served, Carla contacted the station and raised her eyebrows. "Great. Hang on, I'll pass you over to the boss, and you can fill her in."

Carla handed Sara the phone. The waitress deposited their order and left the table.

"Barry, tell me you've located the car?"

"Sort of."

"Meaning what?" Sara picked up her fork and sliced off a piece of cake which in turn toppled and landed on the plate again. She gave up trying to eat one-handed and concentrated on her call instead.

"I've located the car on the CCTV, and yes, I can officially identify Elizabeth Atley as the woman from the hotel with Daly. What I can't do yet is identify the driver."

"Okay, wow, so my gut instinct was right about her. What a bitch. I wonder what her agenda is and where it will end."

"Your guess is as good as mine. One thing I've picked up that's bothering me, boss..."

"Go on."

"I can't say for certain if she's a willing participant or not."

"Okay, well, that's surprising. Are you picking that up from her mannerisms in the car?"

"Yep, they seem pretty distant. Not speaking to one another. Of course, I could be talking out of my arse, like I usually do. I just wanted to put it out there."

"Good man. It's important to cover all the angles. Could this man be forcing her to do things against her will?"

Carla munched on her cake and listened to the conversation with widened eyes.

"Possibly. Will is running the partial plate through the system now. He's drawn a blank so far, but we're hoping to rectify that soon, unless it's a fake plate."

"I wouldn't put it past them. The way this couple are bumping people off, well, they're coming off as sleek professionals. Here's a thing, check the records—you're busy, so allocate the job to one of the girls, if you will. See if anything shows up for someone carrying out crimes like this in the past ten to fifteen years—yes, go with fifteen. Maybe he's got a record and that's what attracted her to him? This could be me talking out of my arse now."

Barry chuckled. "I think we have enough to go on. I'll get back to you with any news."

"Do that. We're in a café, warming up. We'll get on the road again soon."

"Enjoy."

Sara ended the call and passed the mobile back to Carla then tucked into her cake. "Crumbly, isn't it?"

"Delicious, though. Good news on putting Elizabeth at the scene, right?"

"Sort of. Barry seems to think she's none too happy being in the car with the driver."

"Wow! Seriously, as if he's forcing her to torture people? I wonder how she met the bloke."

"Yeah, I'm wondering the same. Maybe things have got out of hand, and now she's eager to put an end to it all. Maybe she has spoken out about it and it's caused a rift between them. Or perhaps it's a case of Barry reading something into it that isn't really there. Hard to tell when observing the CCTV footage sometimes."

"If someone is in a foul mood, I'm sure that would come across in the footage. It would be hard to disguise it, let's say that."

"Camera angles, split-second snapshots, anything could be likely misconstrued, you know that as well as I do. I'd rather keep an open mind on that side of things."

They finished off their brunch and got on the road again. Sara had trouble ditching the feeling that she'd let Emma down.

"What are you thinking?" Carla asked, as if sensing something wasn't quite as it should be.

"It's still bothering me that I didn't do more to protect Emma, especially after what happened to her brother and Bob."

"You're talking nonsense. We've dealt with murders in the past and never felt the need to reach out and offer protection to the other members of the family. You've done nothing wrong this time. I suggest you stop beating yourself up about things."

Sara inhaled a large breath and exhaled it slowly, her mind whirling. "I hear what you're saying, and usually that type of thing wouldn't bug me, so why this time?" She struck the steering wheel with the heel of her hand and hit the siren.

"What the fuck are you doing?" Carla asked, stunned.

"Another thought that doesn't sit comfortably with me. I know the woman has made a complaint about me, but what if she's in danger? Her and the kids? We need to get over there and see if Gail and her family are all right."

Carla crossed her arms tightly. "I think you're making a mistake. Quite frankly, I'd steer clear of this one if I were in your position."

"What harm can it do, taking a drive out there to check on them?" *I'll be risking the chief having a pop at me, but...*

Carla shrugged. "Whatever. Don't blame me if it turns out to be the wrong decision."

"I won't."

Sara drove like a crazed animal and arrived at the mansion within seven minutes. She faced Carla and said, "Are you ready for this?"

Carla waved her can of pepper spray, and Sara flipped open the glove box to retrieve her Taser. "Let's go."

They didn't get far across the drive before Sara realised something was wrong. "Shit! Be careful. Bollocks, I think we're too late."

The front door was ajar.

"Don't say that, it's too soon to think that. One of the kids might have left it open."

Sara rolled her eyes at her partner. "Unlikely. Let's take things nice and slowly, just in case."

Sara's movements were fuelled by anxiety as she approached the house and took the steps one at a time, her stance ready in case someone jumped out on them. She pushed the front door open and strained an ear to listen. Nothing. They entered the house, her guard raised. Sara pointed for Carla to take one side of the hall while she took the other. Between them they pushed open every door and shook their heads when they found the rooms empty. The more they advanced up the hallway, the lower Sara's heart sank. She had been right to come here. When they reached the kitchen, they discovered signs of a struggle. Smashed crockery on the stone floor, and one of the cupboard doors was hanging off its hinges. Had someone tried to hide behind it? One of the kids perhaps?

Sara altered her stance and stood upright. Nothing. "Whoever was here, I think they're long gone."

"And taken the family with them by the look of things. Want me to check upstairs?"

"We'll both do it. I'm going to call it in, get SOCO out here and get this place cordoned off first." Sara placed the call to the station.

Carla wandered through to the pantry and shook her head. "Nothing in there either."

Sara ended the call and placed her phone in her pocket. "Come on, we'll go up together. Safety in numbers and all that."

"Whoever was here—and I think we both know who that is, right? —I think they left a while ago."

"We're on the same wavelength. Let's check anyway, just to be on the safe side."

They carried out the same cautious search upstairs and came to the identical conclusion—the family had been taken against their will.

Sara stomped around the main bedroom, bashing her fist against her thigh. "I let my anger show, and all it's done is made matters worse."

Carla gripped her upper arms and squeezed tight. "Nonsense. I won't let you blame yourself for this."

"Then who is to blame? The family? What for? Grieving and trying to go on with their lives without Alistair Daly? Jesus." She wriggled out of Carla's grip and raked a hand through her hair. Tears pricking, she forced them back.

"We don't know what's gone on yet. Have you got Gail's number?"

Sara pointed at her partner. "Great idea, I'll call her." She tapped in the woman's number she'd found in her notebook, and it rang and rang but remained unanswered. "Damn, well, that tells us fuck all."

"Don't be ridiculous. It tells us far more than if she'd answered the phone."

"I suppose. I'm not coping well with this situation. Maybe you should take over, Carla. The guilt is lying heavy on my shoulders. I've let the family down, and now they're missing."

"You do talk a lot of shit at times. You haven't let anyone down. Stop being so negative. This was out of our control. No one expected the killers to become kidnappers, for fuck's sake, so stop punishing yourself."

"I should've protected them."

"I believe we've had this discussion once already today, I'm not about to repeat myself."

Sara stared at her for a while as she thought. "I'm sorry for melting down."

"Apology accepted, now get your act together. We have a missing family out there somewhere and we need to do all we can to locate them."

Distant sirens alerted them that backup wasn't far away. They decided to retrace their steps and go downstairs to greet them. Sara explained she wanted the house cordoned off as a crime scene and instructed the two uniformed officers to keep everyone out except the SOCO team.

Then Sara and Carla left the mansion and drove back to the station. "You bring the team up to speed, and I'll drop by Price's office. Not that I'm looking forward to it. Hopefully, I won't be long."

They parted at the top of the stairs.

"Good luck." Carla smiled and saluted her.

"Thanks." She was going to need all the luck Carla could bestow upon her and so much more.

Mary, DCI Price's secretary, glanced up from the call she was on and motioned for Sara to take a seat. She declined the offer and paced the area outside the DCI's office.

Mary eventually hung up. "You seem agitated, Sara, can I help?"

"Sorry, I didn't mean to distract you. I need to see the chief on an urgent matter, is she free?"

"I think she is. Let me check." Mary knocked on the chief's door and slipped inside when she was summoned. She emerged and held the door open for Sara to enter.

"Sorry to disturb you, ma'am."

"Take a seat. What's this about, Sara?"

Emotion suddenly overwhelmed her, and she covered her face with her hands. She was determined not to break down, though, so growled and lowered her hands into her lap. "You're not going to like this."

"Fuck, now you're concerning me. Give it to me. What have you done?"

"I haven't done anything wrong...well, not really. Well...maybe I have."

"Ramsey, get to the bloody point," Price demanded sternly.

"Gail Daly and her family have gone missing."

"The woman who put in the complaint? What do you mean they've gone missing?"

"Shit, there's more…we were called out to another murder scene this morning. The victim was Emma Daly, the first victim's sister."

"Holy fucking shit! What are you telling me? That you think the killers have taken the family?"

"I don't know how accurate that is, but yes, it appears to be the case. I've let them all down, and now the killers have abducted Gail and her kids, all because of my bloody-mindedness."

"What have I told you before about leaving any self-pity you might be carrying at the door? Why are you to blame for this? Are you bloody privy to what is going on in the mind of these killers?"

"No, of course not."

"Then why do you persist in blaming yourself? And how the fuck is blaming yourself going to solve this case or get them back? I suggest you leave my office and come back when you're in a better frame of mind."

"I'm sorry. It's just, well…"

"Spit it out. I've never known you to be tongue-tied over the years. What's going on, Sara?"

"I've never had anyone complain about me in the past, and if you want the truth…"

"I do."

"My confidence has been knocked out of me."

Price's features clouded over with anger. "Then you're a blasted idiot. If you were a bloke, I'd order you to grow a pair. Every single copper I know, from constable up to commissioner, has had a complaint made against them at one time or another throughout their career. Don't take my word for it, do some research if you don't believe me. It comes with the territory. You're never going to appease everyone, all of the time. The quicker you get your head around that…"

"I hear you. I've tried to manage my anxieties but I've failed.

Maybe Carla, or even you, should take over the case. As it stands, I think I'm out of my depth."

"What utter bullshit you're spouting. Despite what I implied before I have no intention of ever replacing you in your role. All you need to do is dig into your reserves and show these fuckers who they're frigging dealing with. Christ, Sara, think about what you've achieved over the past year alone. You fought the men who gunned down your husband and rescued your now fiancé from them. What's different about this case?"

She shrugged. She was well aware of what she'd had to contend with over the past year, even longer than that. Was this her body's way of rejecting further conflict, by announcing she wanted to hand the reins over to someone else? If it came down to it, would she be able to take orders from someone else? *I doubt it.*

"Speak to me. What's going on in that head of yours? Am I wrong?"

"No, of course you're not wrong, when are you ever wrong? Maybe I'm tired of dealing with the same shit day in, day out…"

"I'm going to cut you off right there. You're talking more and more shit, and you know what? I'm getting bored with listening to it. Do what you're paid to do, Ramsey. Get off your backside and get out there and find this family."

Sara leapt out of her chair. "Thanks. I'll keep you informed on how things progress."

"You do that. And, Sara."

She reached the door, opened it and turned to face Price. "Yes, boss?"

"You're still the best damn officer I have working under me. Don't let me down."

Sara smiled. "Thanks." If she'd said any more, she would have broken down. She was determined to show her strength, even when she feared it was letting her down at the moment.

Mary winked at her when she left the office. "Chin up, Sara. We all have our bad days. It's how we resolve them that defines us."

"Thanks, Mary."

Sara returned to the incident room with renewed vigour once she'd cast her qualms aside. The team were all hard at it, shouting at each other across the room, their heads bent, staring at their screens.

"What have we got, anything of use?" she asked.

Carla handed Sara a cup of coffee. "I thought you'd need that. How did it go?"

"Fine. She kicked my butt, in a good way this time. Enough about me, what's going on?"

"Barry thinks he's located the owner of the car, a Micky Quaker."

Sara placed her cup on the desk beside her. "Fantastic. We should get over there, to his address."

"Not so fast. We don't think he'll be there."

"What? How?"

Carla motioned for Sara to join her at Barry's desk. "Show her, Barry."

Barry hit a few buttons, and his screen split into four. "I did some checking on the CCTV cameras on the edge of town, close to where the family's mansion is—it was a long shot, I never expected to find anything. But here's the proof that they've got the family." He hit another button.

Sara gasped as a clear image filled the screen. The car, Micky's by all accounts, with four passengers. Three adults and two teenagers in all."

"Shit! My heart's racing here, guys, what does this mean?"

"That's not all," Barry said. "While I was on a roll, I tracked the vehicle to the other side of the town. He's going in the opposite direction to the address we have for him."

"Right. So…he's going to hold them somewhere else?" Sara replied, her mind doing its best to join her heart in the race.

"Yep, I believe so. The bad news is that I lost the car on the outskirts of the town."

"Which direction?"

"North."

"Could he be heading towards Worcester? Or Birmingham maybe? Shit, we need to put out an alert on his car."

"Already done." Carla smiled.

Sara patted her partner on the forearm. "Brilliant, well done, you. Now all we have to do is sit and wait."

Carla puffed out her cheeks. "Or we could get out there ourselves."

"We could. I think it'll likely be a waste of time, though. I think we're better off staying put for now, until someone lays eyes on the vehicle."

The room fell silent for a few moments.

Christine joined them and handed Sara a sheet of paper. "I took the liberty of searching for any possible relatives in the area for Atley and Quaker."

Sara punched her fist in the air and clapped Christine. "Bravo, all of you. You're amazing and have done me proud on this one. Carla, we need to speak to these family members ASAP."

Carla nodded and was already in the process of heaving into her coat.

heir first call was to Atley's parents' house. Sara took a chance they'd be home instead of alerting them by ringing ahead.

Mrs Atley answered the door. "Hello, can I help?"

"Mrs Atley? I'm DI Sara Ramsey, and this is my partner, DS Carla Jameson. Would it be okay if we came in for a quick chat?"

"The police? May I ask what this is concerning?"

Sara glanced over her shoulder at her surroundings and peered through the droplets of rain at the other houses. This was a posh area. Which confused her a little. Facing Mrs Atley again, she said, "Sorry, it's about your daughter."

"My daughter? Which one, I have three?"

Shit! "Umm…Elizabeth."

"What's she been up to now?"

"Mrs Atley, if we could step inside out of the rain, please?"

"Very well. I don't have long. I was on my way to my hair appointment. Will here do?"

"The hallway is fine. Maybe you can tell me when you last saw your daughter?"

"Not for a few weeks, maybe even months. Not since she admitted to having an affair with a married man. I was appalled by her behaviour. We both were. Michael, my husband, has banned her from the house—he was absolutely livid. She's always been the odd one out of the girls. The black sheep in the family, so to speak. Why do you want to know? Is she in trouble?"

"We believe so. Maybe we should take a seat somewhere. What I'm about to tell you might come as a shock."

"Come through to the lounge. Should I ring my husband?"

"Perhaps that would be a good idea. Does he work close by?"

"We're both retired. He's at the golf course. I know, it's raining. He'll be holed up, excuse the pun, in the clubhouse, chin-wagging with his mates, hoping for a break in the weather. I'll ring him now. He'll want to hear what you have to say first-hand." She placed the call. Mr Atley wasn't too happy but agreed to come home all the same.

They waited in silence for him to arrive. Luckily, that turned out to be only a few minutes as the golf club was a stone's throw from their house, which was why they'd moved there a few years before, according to Mrs Atley.

Michael entered the room in what could only be described as Rupert-Bear-type, checked trousers and a waxed jacket that he'd unzipped to reveal a yellow Pringle jumper. "What's the meaning of this intrusion?"

"Now, Michael, calm down, you know what the doctor said about your heart," his wife replied, patting the couch beside her for him to join her.

He removed his jacket, placed it over the back of a chair tucked under a mahogany writing desk off to the left and sat next to his wife. "Get on with it then."

Sara smiled tautly. "We're here to ask you a few questions about Elizabeth, sir."

Michael glanced at his wife and then back at Sara. "What about her?" His brow wrinkled into a deep frown.

"We have reason to believe that she's involved with a man and they've committed some very serious crimes."

He jumped to his feet and paced the room. "I knew she was probably up to no good. She's always the same when she goes off the radar."

"Didn't you ban her from your home, sir?" Sara asked.

"Yes. We'd both had enough of her lies and deceit. My wife and I don't take kindly to finding out one of our daughters had an illicit affair. We haven't spoken to her for maybe two or three months. Sophie will back me up, won't you, love?"

"I'd already hinted at something similar." Sophie seemed agitated, wringing her hands in her lap.

"Has she rung you at all?" Sara probed.

"No. We made it clear that we didn't want anything more to do with her, not while she was with that man. He should be shot for what he's done to his wife and family, shot, I say," Michael said, flinging an arm in the air.

Sara dipped her head a little and prepared herself for what she had to tell them. "The thing is, the man she was seeing called an end to their relationship. Since then, this week, in fact…well, his body was found at the builders' merchants he owned."

Michael fell into the chair next to his wife. All the colour had drained from his face. "I didn't mean to say he should be shot, it was a figure of speech, that's all. I was totally ashamed of what they'd done. Oh God, you're not saying that Elizabeth had a hand in this, are you?"

"That's exactly what I'm saying. It would appear she's met up with a man called Micky Quaker. Does that name mean anything to either of you?"

They both faced each other and shook their heads.

"Okay, I have more to tell you. Alistair isn't the only person we believe they've killed."

Sophie sobbed, and Michael threw an arm around her shoulder.

"No, don't tell me that," Sophie replied.

"I'm afraid so. We're investigating three murders, and they've left a woman with life-changing injuries."

The Atleys were obviously shocked by the news, judging by how tightly they clung to each other.

"One question, why?" Mr Atley muttered, as if saying the word too loud would cause him even more pain.

"We don't really know what the motive is yet, except it obviously has to do with her affair with Alistair."

The couple stared at her in utter disbelief.

"I'm sorry, I can't comprehend this at all," Mrs Atley said. "Yes, Elizabeth has always been a kid who was prone to going off the rails a little, but *murder*? I can't believe she'd stoop to such levels. You mentioned she was involved with another man. Are you sure it's not him carrying out these vile deeds? How can you categorically tell us that Elizabeth has done these dreadful things?"

"I can't. Yes, they're both involved. How they divvy up the crimes, that's what I can't tell you. I want to assure you that she's not personally involved, however, that would be wrong of me to say that. The truth is, none of us know for sure."

"Why aren't you out there looking for them? If they're that dangerous, shouldn't you be doing your best to get them off the street?"

Sara nodded. "Which brings us to why we're here today. We're hoping you can help us."

Mr Atley frowned and shook his head as if to clear his mind. "Sorry? How do you propose we do that, Inspector?"

"I need you to think if she has access to a secret place, perhaps a holiday cottage or a relative's home she was keen on visiting as a child?"

The couple glanced at each other.

"I can't think of anywhere, can you?" Mrs Atley said, wiping her nose on a tissue.

"No, nothing is coming to mind at all. We usually holidayed abroad when the kids were growing up, never in this country."

Sara's heart plummeted. "What about relatives who live close by, anything coming to mind there? A favourite aunt or uncle perhaps."

Mr Atley firmly shook his head. "No, nothing at all. All our relatives are down south, in the Devon area, none around here."

"It's a long shot, but would you mind giving me their addresses?"

"If we have to, but I think you'll be wasting your time. It's not as if Elizabeth is close to anyone else in our family. She was always quite a loner as a child. Whenever someone came to visit, she tended to stay in her room most of the time and only appear at mealtimes."

"We'd like the addresses all the same, just in case."

Mrs Atley left her seat and searched in her handbag which she collected from the other side of the room. Carla stood and offered the woman her notebook to jot down the information while Sara continued the conversation with Mr Atley.

"What about her sisters, is she likely to visit them?"

"I don't think so, they've barely spoken to each other since it all came out."

"Do they live locally?"

"One in Worcester, the other around the corner from here."

"Could we also have the Worcester address?"

Mrs Atley nodded. "I'll get that for you."

Sara noticed the woman's hand shaking as she wrote the information in Carla's notebook.

"I'm sorry this is so distressing for you. I regret coming here and putting you through this." She felt obligated to apologise. The last thing she wanted was another complaint against her. *Is this how it's going to be from now on? Me checking and double-checking my actions in case I offend anyone? Sod that for a lark.*

"What do you know about this man?" Mr Atley asked.

"Nothing much at the moment, his name has only just surfaced. My team is looking into his background as we speak. I felt it was imperative to come and see you as soon as possible rather than hang around at the station, twiddling our thumbs."

"I suppose that makes sense." He ran a hand through his hair. "I can't quite believe what you've told us. It's refusing to sink in. To think a daughter of mine could be guilty of taking someone's life."

Sara sighed. "There's something I haven't told you. The reason we're keen to track them down is because we believe they've kidnapped Alistair's family. His wife and two children."

"Oh my God," Mr Atley shouted. "Bloody hell, why? Don't tell me they're going to kill them as well?"

"Honestly, your guess is as good as mine."

"It doesn't make sense. Why kidnap the family? Are they hoping to get some form of ransom out of other family members?"

"Again, I can't answer that. As far as we know, Alistair only had a brother and sister. Unfortunately, his sister was killed by Elizabeth and this man yesterday. Not long after we attended the crime scene, we discovered the family had been kidnapped."

"This sounds like one of those B-movies. I am genuinely lost for words."

Carla and Mrs Atley returned to their seats once their task had been completed.

"Okay, then I'm going to suggest we leave things there for now. I'll give you one of my cards. Please ring me if you happen to hear from her."

"What if we do? Shall we tell her that you're closing in on her? That is how you say it, isn't it?"

Sara stood and glanced down at the man. "You can tell her that we'd like to speak to her and give her my number, if you would."

Mr Atley showed Sara and Carla to the front door, leaving the sobbing Mrs Atley behind in the lounge.

Sara shook the man's hand. "I'm sorry for the distress we've caused today."

"We'll get over it. What we'll never get over is knowing that our daughter is a murderer. That's going to be bloody tough to get used to, Inspector."

"I can understand that, sir. Try not to dwell on it too much, we don't really know the accuracy behind that statement just yet."

"You mean, you're thinking this is more about him than her? Are you telling me Elizabeth could be in danger?"

Sara shrugged, annoyed with herself for opening her mouth again. "Who knows? We'll be in touch soon if we get any news."

"We'll do the same if she contacts us, you have my word on that. I refuse to harbour a criminal, even if she is my own daughter."

"That's good to hear, sir."

They left the house and jumped back into the car. Sara pulled away from the kerb. Once they were out of sight of the house, she drew the vehicle to a halt and switched off the engine.

"We need to get on to the station, see what they've found out about Quaker." She withdrew her phone from her pocket. "Hi, Barry, it's me. Any news on Quaker?"

"I was about to ring you, boss. Yep, not good news. He's been in prison on GBH charges, two of them. The most recent one, the guy ended up in hospital and was paralysed. He got four years for that."

"Shit! When did he get out?"

"At the beginning of last year."

"Bloody hell, I wonder if Elizabeth realised who she was getting involved with," Sara said, more to herself than anyone else.

"I stand by what I said earlier, boss. My take is that she doesn't seem at all happy with how things are going. Maybe he's got some kind of a hold over her."

"Either way, we're scrabbling around trying to find them and are no sodding further forward."

"I'll keep searching the CCTV and ANPR cameras, boss. I believe it's the only way we're going to locate them."

"You do that. Keep me informed. Carla and I are going to call at Quaker's parents' house, see what we can dig up there, if anything. I'm not going to hold my breath, though. Then we'll head back to base, unless we hear anything else from you guys in the meantime."

"Rightio."

Sara tucked her phone back in her pocket and blew out a discouraged breath.

"Keep a clear mind about this. We're doing our best."

Sara faced her partner. "It's not good enough, is it? I'm full of dread at the moment. Aware of what they've done to the other people, it's pretty obvious what their intentions are. We have to find them, Carla, but *how*? If someone truly doesn't want to be found, then how are we supposed to get around that?"

"By remaining focused at all times. A break will come our way soon enough, it usually does."

"You're right. Our main priority is to keep positive. Let's see what his parents have to say, and then I'm going to have to call a press conference."

"That comes with its own risks, as you know."

"What else can we do?"

9

*E*lizabeth was just as scared as Gail and her two kids. They had arrived at the derelict farmhouse thirty minutes before. Elizabeth already detested her surroundings even more than she hated Micky right now, and that was saying something.

He caught her off guard and flung an arm around her shoulders. "What's up, babe? You look down in the mouth."

"I'm fine. Tired, that's all."

"We'll soon be able to get away from it all. Once we get rid of our excess baggage, if you get my drift." He laughed and squeezed her shoulder with his strong grip, encouraging her to do the same.

She lowered her voice so the others couldn't hear. "What are you going to do with them?"

He tapped his nose. "I've got plans. Something that's going to make your toes curl."

"Why? Why do it to the kids? They've got nothing to do with this, Micky."

"They've got *everything* to do with this. They'll be the first to go—it'll be extra cool to let the mother suffer even more."

Elizabeth knew better than to react. She turned to him and smiled.

"That's my girl. You'll get used to this, even come to enjoy it, in the end. I think you got a thrill out of burning that bitch Emma, didn't you? Admit it?"

She nodded. What else could she do? Her gaze drifted over to the family, huddled together, sitting on the dusty floor of the old kitchen. The cupboards had been ripped out long before, and all that remained were piles of dust and the old pipework, otherwise there was nothing to say what this room had been used for in the past. Gail's gaze latched on to hers. At first there was a determination in her blue eyes; now there was nothing but fear emanating from them.

"They'll need feeding. I should've picked up supplies on the way here. Food and drink, we'll all need that. How long are you intending to stay here?" Elizabeth asked.

"However long it takes. What's with all the questions?"

"Well, we haven't discussed any of this, so I haven't got a clue what's expected of me."

"You're expected to tend to their needs, and mine." He planted a wet kiss on her cheek.

She fought hard to suppress the urge to vomit. *How long will this go on? What can I do to change things, for them and for me? I can't allow him to hurt them—no, I won't allow him. But if I do anything against his wishes, he's going to turn the tables on me and...no, I can't think about that. I need to help these poor people, they don't deserve to be caught up in this. I feel so guilty that things have gone this far. The knife...I forgot I had that.*

She concentrated hard, not wishing to openly touch her sleeve to see if it was still there. She could feel it, at least she thought she could.

"Right, we need to get them secured. I'll help you do that and then I'll search the garage et cetera, see what I can find out there to heat this damn place."

"Maybe we're doing it all wrong. Why come here?"

He clutched her chin in his hand and glared at her. "Are you doubting me?"

"No, I'd never do that. Look around us, Micky, this place is a tip."

"It suits my needs." He flung her head to the side and let go. "We're wasting time, let's tie them up."

Together, with the use of the tow rope from the car, they secured the three members of Alistair's family. Lydia was crying pitifully, pleading for them not to hurt her.

Micky slapped her around the face. "Shut the fuck up, you snivelling bitch."

"Please, don't hurt my kids. Do what you like to me, but don't hurt either of them," Gail begged.

Micky rested his forehead against Gail's and sneered. "You might be able to boss them around, but don't think that'll work on me, got that?"

"Yes, I'm sorry. Tell us what you want from us."

"You'll find out soon enough." He smacked Gail's forehead with his own.

She cried out in pain, and he laughed.

Elizabeth closed her eyes, hoping to block out the family's misery. She opened them again to find him barely six inches in front of her.

He jabbed her in the chest a few times. "I'm not liking what I'm seeing. What's wrong with you?"

"Nothing. I'm not feeling too well. I need food, I feel faint."

He held his hand against her stomach. "Is it the baby?"

Gail gasped on the other side of the room. Elizabeth's gaze darted in her direction. She hadn't wanted the woman to find out. Not like this.

She returned her attention to Micky and stroked his face. "I'll nip to the shop, see what I can find."

"No. You stay here. I'll go, once I've found something to heat this place."

"Okay. The temperature is dropping rapidly. Do you want me to search the house? There could be some old furniture here we could burn."

"Good idea. They're secure now, they won't be going anywhere. I'll be back soon." He kissed her hard on the mouth.

As tempted as she was to turn away from his advance, she resisted. Instead, she smiled and watched him leave the room. She put a finger to her lips, ensuring Gail didn't speak. The door banged, and Elizabeth let out a relieved sigh.

She approached the family. "I'm sorry you're in this situation."

Gail looked her in the eye and asked, "You're pregnant? Whose is it? Alistair's?"

Elizabeth nodded. "Yes. I didn't want any of this. I'm in over my head."

"You have to help us. What are his intentions? To kill us?"

"I don't know. I'm going to do what I can." She removed the knife from her sleeve. "I have this. I'll use it on him if I have to."

"Or you could use it to set us free. We could make a run for it, me and the children. I know you want to help us. Do this for us, please?"

"I can't. Not while he's still here. You heard him, he'll be going out to the shop soon. I'll pretend to be ill. He'll do what I want then, I hope."

"He seems to care deeply about the baby. Does he think it's his?" Gail asked.

Elizabeth bit down on her lip. "I had to tell him that, otherwise he would've killed it. If he ever finds out...he'll kill me for lying to him."

"It's okay, your secret is safe with us. Please, don't let him hurt my children."

"I'll do my best. Stay quiet. I need to search for furniture. Know that I'm on your side and that I regret everything that has happened so far."

"I believe you."

Elizabeth set off. She travelled through the damp house and noticed that a few of the windows were broken in some of the rooms. She pulled across the green, moth-eaten velour curtains still in situ to try to prevent the draught filtering into the other rooms. There was no furniture downstairs. Upstairs was a different story. There she found a wooden bedframe with a soiled mattress in the main bedroom. The others contained several pieces of furniture, a chest of drawers in the second bedroom, and in the box room stood a wardrobe from the thirties. There was no way she'd be able to carry them down the creaking staircase, not without risking the baby.

The door banged downstairs. "Elizabeth, where are you?" Micky shouted.

"I'm up here. I've found some furniture we can use. You'll need to help me bring it down, though."

He appeared in the doorway of the main bedroom. "Good girl. This should keep the house warm for the next few days at least."

"What then? Are we going to leave? We'll have to, won't we?"

He darted forward and grasped her around the throat. "There you go again with the questions. What's with you?"

She held her hands to her stomach. "The baby, Micky."

He released his grip and followed it up with a kiss. "I'm sorry. Why do you persist in trying my patience? Questioning everything I do?"

Because you're a psycho! "I'm not. All I did was ask what you intend to do next. I apologise for being curious. I'll keep quiet from now on."

"No, don't do that. Sorry, I'm on edge."

"Why?"

"I have plans for the family, daring plans that I need to put into action. Bear with me, that could take a day or two to pull together."

Elizabeth was determined not to let on how nervous she was, scared even, for the family. "Okay, let me know what I can do to help."

"I will, babe, when the time is right. Are you up to helping me lift some of this stuff downstairs?"

"I'm not sure, I'm worried the heavy lifting will hurt the baby. Why don't we get the boy to help?"

"What?" He paused to think the suggestion over and then nodded. "Okay, I don't think that's such a bad idea after all. I'll go and get him. You stay here, you can assist by giving us directions, how's that?"

"Sounds perfect to me. Anything to keep this little one safe," she replied, milking the situation that was clearly keeping his temper under control.

he elderly couple were beside themselves. The more Sara explained about the situation, the more they shook their heads and clung to each other.

"We can't help you, Inspector. Please don't tar us with the same brush. That boy lost the plot years ago. We tried to seek help for him through the usual channels, and nothing, absolutely zero help came our way. After his first spell in prison he changed. I've always wondered if prison altered people for the worse, not the better. In Micky's case that was certainly true. He hung around with the lowest of the low; he openly bragged about it when he got out the first time. He told us they taught him things which would make him powerful in the area."

"Powerful?" Sara asked.

Mr Quaker nodded. "Bizarre, right? I questioned him about what he meant by that, and all he told me was to watch and learn. Well, we watched all right, and all we learnt was that once he came into contact with anyone he knew, they instantly fell under his spell. We're ashamed to say that he terrorised our neighbourhood. Everyone fell out with us."

"They blamed you for his crimes?"

"Yes, I suppose, because when he was released from prison that first time, we took him back. We regretted our actions after about a week." His head lowered, and his wife reached for a tissue to dab at the tears falling.

"May I ask why?"

"It's difficult for both of us. Sooty was a treasured pet, she didn't deserve to die like that. At the hands of a…"

Sara held a hand to her chest. "Are you telling me he killed one of your pets?"

"Our cat. He not only killed her…he tortured her. Laughed about it to our faces as we buried her in the back garden. We knew then how far he'd strayed off the rails. I kicked him out that day. He couldn't believe it. Never apologised for killing Sooty, merely shrugged and packed a bag, as if he didn't have a clue that he'd done anything wrong. I have to say we haven't missed him, not after what he did. What kind of sick mind would do that to an innocent creature? All the help in the Western Hemisphere couldn't have helped that lad, I'm pretty damn sure about that."

Sara heaved out a sigh and revealed the true reason behind their visit.

Mrs Quaker sniffled and said quietly, "And to think, that man came from my womb. It makes me want to vomit just thinking about it. He used to be such a pleasant boy. One bad incident in town one night sent him on the path of self-destruction, which in turn, led him on the path of evil. I'll never forgive him, never. I refuse to feel guilty about that."

"I don't think anyone would blame you, Mrs Quaker. I'm sorry that people in authority failed to listen to you. Prison occasionally brings out the worst in people."

"It's something that's taught in there, or so he said. Oh God, I can't even bring myself to say my own child's name."

Mr Quaker stroked his wife's arm. "There, there, love. It's over now, try not to upset yourself. He'll never be allowed to step foot in the house, not as long as there's a breath left in this knackered, worn-out body of mine."

"And what happens then? If you die before me? How will I keep him out?" Turning to Sara, she said, "You need to find him and bury the ruddy key this time. The boy is insane."

"Did you report what he did?" Sara asked.

"To the cat?" Mr Quaker asked. Sara nodded. "What was the point? They wouldn't have done anything."

Sara had a feeling that was where Micky's torture tendencies had derived from, his own back yard. She dreaded to think how much the cat had suffered at this warped individual's hands, after seeing his recent techniques. *How many more cats have suffered at his hands over the years?* Sara was aware that most serial killers had something lacking in their genetic makeup, setting them aside from 'normal people' as it were. "I'm sorry you didn't come to us back then. Maybe we would've been able to get the help he needed, had we known about the dreadful incident."

"If that comment was supposed to make us feel guilty, Inspector, well, it doesn't. As I said, we've done our best by the lad over the years. I'm sorry he's evading you now. All I'd suggest is to get as many men as possible to help with the hunt. My wife and I refuse to have anything to do with this as we disowned the lad."

"All we're trying to find out is if you might know of anywhere he might be using as a hideaway. Somewhere he used to visit as a child perhaps?"

"I can't think of anywhere. Don't you think after all we've told you that we would tell you? We're heartbroken for this family, however, we refuse to feel guilty. We turned our backs on the boy years ago, aware how it would likely end. No one went out of their way to help us. They're to blame for this outcome, not us."

"I understand how let down you must feel, Mr and Mrs Quaker. Okay, we'll leave things there. If, by any chance, he comes to visit you, may I leave you a card for you to contact me?"

Mr Quaker took the card and showed them to the front door. "Of course we will. I hope you find the family before it's too late."

Sara shook his hand. "So do we. I apologise if our visit has opened up old wounds, sir. I never meant for that to happen."

"What's done is done. We should have moved house years ago,

then you wouldn't have been able to trace us. I only hope he hasn't got the same idea."

"Why didn't you move?"

"Barbara loves it here. Says the neighbours are wonderful and she dreaded the thought of starting afresh and ending up with bad ones."

"I see. Thanks for your time."

"Good luck." He closed the door gently behind them.

On the walk back to the car, Carla said, "I feel sorry for them, they're clearly distraught about begetting an evil prick."

"Begetting? My heart goes out to them, but speaking to them hasn't truly helped our investigation. It was pretty bloody obvious we're searching for a deranged killer—make that killers."

"So, what's next?"

"There's only one thing left to do: seek the help of the media and the general public. Yes, doing that could likely work against us and put the family in even more jeopardy but, bloody hell, how else are we going to find them before he chooses to end their effing lives?"

They dropped into their seats and attached their seat belts.

"I hear you. It's a risk we're being forced to take. Someone must've seen them."

"Will you make all the arrangements, or ring the press officer to deal with it, while I drive?"

"Yep, consider it done."

By the time they arrived at the station, everything had been actioned, and Sara had two hours to prepare for the conference. She hated doing them, always suffered from a little stage fright, but they were a necessary evil in most investigations.

*T*wo hours later, her nerves set aside for the duration, she put out her plea to the good people of Hereford. She wondered if anyone in the crowd noticed how tightly she had her fingers crossed during the appeal. The usual questions came at her, thick and fast, during the media circus which lasted approximately thirty minutes. Once she'd thanked the journalists for attending, she returned to the incident room and waited, along with the rest of the team, for the phones to ring with any possible leads as to the wanted couple's whereabouts.

The first few calls they received were your usual run-of-the-mill-type of calls they got every time a plea was issued by the police. All the information was noted down and added to the pile. Sara was intrigued when she circulated the room and overheard Marissa speaking to someone.

"When was this, sir?" Marissa asked the caller.

Sara bent down to eavesdrop in on the conversation. "A few hours or more. It looked like the car anyway, although I could be mistaken. There were definitely a lot of adults in the car, that's what struck me as odd really."

Sara gave Marissa the thumbs-up.

Marissa nodded and continued with her conversation. "If you can give me as much detail as possible, sir."

Sara walked away and glanced over the shoulders of the rest of the team at the notes they'd taken. Once Marissa had finished her call, Sara appealed for everyone's attention. A few of them ended the calls they were on, if the information was leading them nowhere.

"Okay, it looks like we've got a hit of sorts. Marissa, would you like to fill the rest of us in?"

"The gentleman I spoke to said he'd spotted a car fitting the description of Quaker's down a country lane, close to Much Cowarne. There appeared to be a number of adults in the car, which raised his suspicions. That's about it, boss."

"It's better than nothing. Who fancies taking a trip out there to have a nose around?"

Will and Barry both raised their hands.

"That's settled then. See what you can find out. Knock on a few doors if you have to. I'm not sure how densely populated that area is, but do your best."

"I think the houses are spaced out around there, boss," Will replied, slipping on his jacket.

"That could prove pivotal to the investigation. We'll let you know if anything else comes our way in the interim."

The two men left the room. Sara headed for the vending machine and shouted the rest of the team a coffee. She was eager for a caffeine fix herself. After handing the drinks around, she took hers into the office to tackle the paperwork she'd neglected to process that morning. She'd been lax with that particular task all week. It didn't stop her mind from drifting to Gail and her family's plight, and once again the nagging doubts of how she'd handled the situation took root in her stomach. She offered up a silent prayer. She wasn't really a religious person, not to that extent, but this was an emergency. She prayed for the family's safety and also that someone would ring in soon with valuable information as to where Quaker and Atley were keeping them.

By the time she'd sieved through the paperwork, she was in dire need of hearing a friendly voice, so she rang Mark. "Hi, can you talk?"

"Of course I can. Let me put this hamster in its cage and I'll be with you." Metal clattered shut in the background, and then Mark was back on the line. "How's things?"

"So-so. I needed to hear your voice."

"Anything I can help with?"

"Not really. The case is driving me potty. At the moment we're chasing our damn tails more than finding anything substantial to cling on to."

"Sorry to hear that, love. Will you be home the usual time this evening?"

"You know what? I'd feel like a shit if I deserted the team so early. We have a family in mortal danger, and I think I should be here in case anything breaks."

"I get that, but you're also going to need to get some rest, love. Why don't I drop by the station later and take you out for a pub meal? That way you'll still be on hand except for, say, half an hour."

"You're adorable to think of me. In all honesty, I'm not sure my stomach will take a huge meal."

"Then don't have one. Have a jacket spud instead. Come on, you have to eat. You'll be no good to anyone if you don't."

She chuckled. "That's typical of you, always thinking of your stomach. Saying that, Carla and I stopped off to bolt down coffee and a slice of cake to keep us going. All right, you win. See you around seven then? Can we go to the pub opposite?"

"Makes sense. See you then. Chin up, Sara, you've got this. I love you."

"I wish I had your confidence. I love you, too." She ended the call with a smile on her face, finished up her paperwork and returned to the incident room.

Carla signalled for Sara to join her. She replaced the phone in the docking station. "That was an interesting one. A barmaid at The White Swan said she knows Quaker quite well."

"Right, you've got my attention. How? From working at the pub?"

"Yep. She admitted to having a crush on him for a while. Before he took up with Elizabeth, he used to brag about having his eye on this derelict farm out in the sticks. He had this grand notion of doing the place up and getting married, raising a family even."

Sara perched on the desk behind her. "Wow, does that sound like the same character to you?"

"He sounds psychotic to me. Do you think that's why he targeted Elizabeth, saw her as a way of fulfilling his dreams? Is that what this is all about?"

"Maybe. All right, perhaps he expected to find more money in the safe at the builders' merchants the night he tortured Alistair, maybe that pissed him off."

Carla snapped her fingers. "The family. They're the only thing left. The only opportunity to take the family for money, it could be why he's chosen to kidnap them."

Sara placed her thumb and forefinger around her chin. "You're thinking the insurance money?"

"Exactly. It makes sense."

"It does, except I doubt any insurance company would pay out if a family was being held hostage for the funds, would they? I've never come across this type of scenario before. Will you ring a company, get the lowdown on that for me, Carla?"

Her partner picked up the phone and dialled a number. Within seconds she had the answer. "Nope, they won't pay out in those circumstances. I can kind of understand their logic behind that, although, it's not going to help family members in that situation."

The phone rang on Carla's desk. She answered it, cringed and put the caller on hold. "Jesus, we forgot all about him."

"Who?"

"Des Daly. He's absolutely furious because he found out through the media that Gail and the kids have been kidnapped."

"Fuck, my bad. Okay, put the call through to my office. I'll suffer the consequences and his wrath in private."

"Will do. Good luck."

Sara sucked in a number of calming breaths as she walked towards her office. She had to play this just right, not sound too downbeat or too bright when she spoke to him. "Hi, Mr Daly, this is DI Ramsey."

"Well, it's about bloody time. How dare you keep me waiting? Now, do you mind telling me why you haven't bothered to inform me that my family have been kidnapped? Why I had to find out about it along with every other Tom, Dick and Harry in the blasted area?"

"I'm sorry. As you can imagine, after I conducted the conference, the phonelines have been ringing off the hook, and no, that's not an excuse. It was unforgiveable of me not to get in touch with you, especially after what happened to your brother and Emma."

"Exactly my point. This is bloody ridiculous. You had a duty to tell me and you've neglected to do it. Where is the rest of my family, do you know?"

"We've had a few good hits from the calls coming in. We're in the process of piecing it all together now."

"Meaning what? Do you know where they're being kept? Are you planning to storm the place and get them back before this maniac strikes again with his fucking instruments of torture and kills them all?"

"As I've already stated, we're piecing valuable information together. We have to be certain of the situation before we go rushing in there and mess things up. You wouldn't want that, would you?" she asked, turning the tables on him.

"No, all I want is for you to do your damn job and keep me informed. Don't you think this family has suffered enough this week? My poor parents don't know what's frigging hit them. Get the bastard and rescue the rest of my family or..."

"Or? You think making threats is going to help matters, Mr Daly?"

"I'm sorry. I went too far. I'd like to think you'd be considerate of my frustrations at this stressful time."

"All I can say is that my team and I are doing our best. We'll be working around the clock on this investigation until we capture the bastard, of that you can be assured."

"Thank you. I'm sorry for venting my anger. You didn't deserve that."

"Maybe I did. Please, forgive me for not contacting you, that was remiss of me and won't happen again. Pass on my reassurance to your parents and my condolences for losing Emma. I should have rung them, I didn't."

"I will. Let's draw a line under this for now. I appreciate you're doing all you can to capture the killers."

"Sounds good to me. I'll ring you if I hear anything, I promise." She ended the call and leaned back, unexpected tears of frustration forming. *Why am I messing things up? The simplest of tasks, and I'm damn well neglecting my duties. Why?*

Carla walked in a few minutes later and found her in the same position. "Thought I'd pop in, see if everything is all right. Do you need to chat about anything?"

Sara sat forward and smiled at her partner. "Not really, I'm just going over things in my head. I'm even more determined to catch the buggers this evening, if we can. Des is right, I've let them all down, I need to make amends."

Carla tutted. "You've done nothing of the sort, and I won't allow you to beat yourself up about this, Sara. I take it Des was livid?"

"Livid, irate, furious...all of the above and so much more besides. Can you do me a favour? Check with the team, see who's up for some overtime tonight. If they are, we'll need to sort out what to do about dinner. Mark is meeting me in the pub over the road at seven—we could do it in shifts to go over there, or ring up for takeaway, it's up to you guys. I'll only be out thirty minutes."

"You deserve a break. I'll ask the others what they want to do. Umm...I did some extra digging on Quaker. His actual rap sheet is longer than we first thought: GBH, ABH and possession of a firearm."

"Great, another snippet of information that has brightened my day, not. Okay, by that, we have to consider that he has contacts in the underworld, yes?"

"That's how I'm reading it. The question is, are these guys local? They might be from Birmingham or Worcester. Perhaps they're holed up somewhere for the night with the intention of moving further north tomorrow."

"Sounds reasonable. Has this really only been going on a few days? It seems like it's been dragging on for weeks, if not months."

"I hope we can bring it to a swift conclusion, for the family's sake."

"I'll second that."

Carla left the room, and Sara got back to her boring paperwork with a renewed vigour to get it out of the way.

11

"*A*ll right. You have a point. I'll release the boy; he can help me bring the furniture down." Micky trundled downstairs and returned with the Daly boy a few moments later. The boy appeared nervous. His hands shook as he lifted the bottom of the wardrobe when Micky tilted it.

Elizabeth tried to reassure the lad. "It's heavy. I know you can do it, though."

"I'll do my best. Dad never used to ask me to do this type of thing around the house. I'm not very strong."

"It's about time you learnt what a man's role in this life is then, boy. Put your back into it," Micky shouted. "I'll go first, take most of the weight. Elizabeth, you stay with the lad, make sure he does his fair share."

"I will. I'll lend a hand if I have to."

"No, don't you dare. Be careful of the baby."

The wardrobe was manoeuvred into position with Micky going backwards down the stairs, taking the strain.

"It's Ross, isn't it?" Elizabeth asked the boy.

His eyes narrowed, and he nodded. "That's right."

"Don't worry, you'll be fine. I'll be here to guide you."

He nodded and shuffled his feet along the landing to the top step. The wardrobe was tilting at a severe angle now. Elizabeth peered over the top. Micky's head could only just be seen. It was then an idea sparked in Elizabeth's mind. She reached for the wardrobe and gave it a shove.

Ross glared at her. "What are you doing?" he whispered.

She winked at him as Micky shouted, "What the fuck was that? Hold it steady, squirt."

"His hand slipped. It's all right, we're sorted at this end now," Elizabeth replied. She inhaled a steadying breath and mouthed to the boy, "Trust me."

He nodded.

They got to about a third of the way down the staircase when Elizabeth shoved the wardrobe again, with a lot more strength this time.

Ross played along with her. "Oh no, I can't hold it any longer…"

He let go, and Micky was sent toppling backwards with the wardrobe following him.

Elizabeth watched on, her fingers tightly crossed down by her side, hoping he would soon be squished under the heavy furniture.

Micky cursed and shouted, and then everything went quiet. Elizabeth and Ross stared at each other and then back at Micky. They inched their way one step at a time and squeezed past the wardrobe. Micky was lying prostrate on the floor, buried beneath.

"Get this fucking thing off me. Ouch! I think my leg is busted."

Elizabeth's heart rate multiplied. She was winging this now, had no idea what to do for the best. All she knew was that she had to get this family out of here. She shoved Ross away from her and screeched, "Run. Go now. Get help!"

"I can't leave Mum and Lydia, don't make me do that."

"Go, it's your only chance"

"Elizabeth, what the fuck? You let that kid go and…it'll be the last thing you do on this earth. Baby or no baby, I'll string you up in the barn."

Elizabeth drew back her foot and kicked Micky in the face. Then she pushed Ross towards the front door, urging him to leave.

The poor kid was confused. She could tell he was in two minds about leaving his mum and sister.

"They'll be fine. I'll watch over them. Go get help, please? Run!"

"Do it, Ross," his mother shouted, tears glistening on her cheeks.

With that, Ross bolted out of the door. Elizabeth walked over to where Micky was lying on the floor. He had managed to shift the heavy wardrobe a little. Elizabeth's hands became sweaty, and she was at a loss what to do next to help save this family. It looked like Micky was digging into his reserves to find the strength to aid himself. All of a sudden, he let out a rallying cry and heaved the wardrobe to one side. He reached out for the newel post to help him get to his feet.

He scowled at her. "What the fuck? I never thought I'd see the day when you'd turn against me. You're going to be sorry you did that, bitch." He hobbled a few paces.

She stumbled backwards, out of his grasp, and then his annoyance fuelled his movements and he lunged at her. She yelped as his fingers dug into her arms. He took a swing, and his fist connected with her stomach.

She doubled over, the pain excruciating—she'd never felt pain like it before. "No, please, don't hurt my baby." *The knife...I must get the knife.*

Her plea went unheard. He kept raining blows down on her, one after the other until she could stand no more and passed out.

*S*ara had enjoyed her meal with Mark. It was a tad frantic but worth it. The lasagne and chips would see her through the night, if necessary. "I need to get back. I really appreciate you coming to see me, love." She kissed her fiancé, a long salty kiss.

"Be safe out there."

"I will."

They parted at the entrance to the pub. Sara ran across the road and in through the station's front door.

"Please, please, you have to help me."

"Take a seat and wait your turn, lad, can't you see I'm dealing with this lady?" Jeff, the desk sergeant, said, dismissing the lad.

Sara peered at the boy and gasped. "Shit! Ross, is that you?"

The boy broke down in tears. She reached out and wrapped her arms around him. "You're safe. Come with me. Sergeant, open the door. This is Ross Daly, the lad we've been looking for."

"What the heck? I'm sorry, ma'am, I had no idea." He buzzed the door open.

Sara led Ross up the stairs to the incident room.

"Do you want a coffee?" she asked, guiding him to the nearest chair.

"No. I just want my mum and my sister. You have to help them."

"Gather around, folks. This is Ross Daly."

The team all swivelled in their chairs to look at the lad.

"Please, we haven't got time for this. Mum and Lydia are in danger. He's mad. You have to help me."

"Okay, I need you to try and remain calm and tell us what you know. How did you get here?"

"He kidnapped us and took us to this awful farmhouse. No one has lived there for years. The woman, she said she used to be my dad's girlfriend. I don't know about that…she tried to help us. I escaped, she helped me. I ran until I reached the road. I was so scared, it's pitch-black out there. A car came past, and I flagged it down, pleaded with the driver to bring me here. We need to get to them. He's going to hurt them. You have to help me."

"We will. Would you be able to guide us to this farmhouse?"

"Of course. We have to go."

"Okay, if this man is as dangerous as we think he is, we're going to need to call for backup. Carla, get on to the Armed Response Team. Marissa, contact Will for me, he's out that way. Tell him to stay where he is and apprise him of the situation."

Both women nodded and jumped into action.

"You're safe, Ross. Hang in there, we'll get your mother and sister out of this, I promise. Can you tell us if this man has any weapons?"

"I don't know. He went outside, said he was tinkering in a barn. I haven't got a clue what he was saying or doing."

"What about Elizabeth? You said she helped you escape. Have they fallen out?"

"She's scared. Umm...she's pregnant and was trying to protect the baby. She helped me push the wardrobe we were shifting on top of him. We were moving it downstairs to use as firewood. There's no heating in the house. It's a mess, cold and damp."

"She's pregnant. Wow, okay, we weren't aware of that."

"My mum asked her if it was my dad's." He scratched the side of his head. "I'm confused. I don't know what's going on. I loved my dad, and now all this stuff is coming out about him. Why?"

"We're as much in the dark about things as you are, love. I'm sure everything will be explained properly soon. Don't think badly of your dad."

"What? Why shouldn't I? He cheated on Mum with this woman— she's half Mum's age. Old enough to be my sister. Makes me want to puke."

Sara rubbed the top of his arm. "Your mum will be able to explain things better once all this is over. For now, let's concentrate on getting you all back together."

"I'd like that. How long before we can get out there?"

Carla joined them again. "ART will be good to go in thirty minutes."

"Crikey! Let's hope that's not too long. Ross, how long is it since you escaped the farmhouse?"

He shrugged. "I don't know, about forty minutes, I didn't bother to check my watch."

"That's fine, don't worry."

Marissa joined the group. "Will has pulled over and is awaiting further instructions, boss. They haven't managed to locate anything while they've been out."

"No problem. I think this place would be hard to find."

"Umm... I think I've found a possible farm, boss," Christine shouted behind her.

Sara swiftly turned and crossed the room to the constable's desk. "Show me."

"Here. I used all the information we had and pulled up a map of the area. On the satellite images, this place stuck out like a sore thumb."

Sara patted her on the shoulder. "Good work, Christine. Ross, can you come here?"

The lad appeared beside Sara soon after. He peered at the screen. Christine had blown up the image of the farmhouse in the hope he'd recognise it.

"Is this the place?"

He squinted at the screen. Christine showed the building from different angles.

"I only saw it from the front. It might be. Hang on, it's close to the church, we passed that on the way there. Yes, I'm sure it's the place."

"Brilliant news. Well done, you. Marissa, ring Will back, give him the coordinates. Tell him to find the farmhouse and keep it under observation until we get there. Lights off, of course, we wouldn't want to arouse this guy's suspicion."

"I'll get on to him now, boss." She ran back to her seat and placed the call.

Sara steered Ross back to his chair. "You're doing well. Don't worry, Ross, we'll get them back."

"I hope I haven't made it worse for them, you know, by running off."

"I doubt it. Keep thinking positively. I'm going to take you back downstairs now, get the desk sergeant to look out for you while I get on the road. Are you okay with that?"

He shook his head. "No, I want to come with you. Please, I need to make sure my family are okay."

Sara chewed on her lip and finally relented. "Okay, but once we're there, you've got to promise me, no matter what goes down, that you'll stay in the car until it's over."

"I promise. Can we go now?"

Sara placed a hand on his cheek. "Soon. Just be patient."

. . .

*T*en minutes later, Sara, Carla and Ross all piled into the car. She'd received notification from the ART leader that the team was en route to the farmhouse. Will had already made contact, telling her that he and Barry were in position, a few yards from the entrance to the farmhouse. Sara had warned them not to react until they arrived, to observe only.

Ross was totally silent on the journey. The radio sprang into life now and again with an update from the ART unit. Everything was moving so fast, Sara hoped the lad didn't get overwhelmed by it all and mess up when they got there.

Carla pointed ahead. "Will's car."

Sara had already switched off the lights and glided to a halt behind the other members of her team. Then they were forced to wait until the ART joined them. Sara had already advised them to approach without lights. She saw the vehicle pull up behind her and stepped out of the car to speak to the commanding officer.

"Get back in the car. Leave this to us, Inspector. We'll come and fetch you when the danger has been eliminated."

"Thanks." What else could she say to that? She slipped back behind the steering wheel and heaved out a couple of impatient sighs the more they were forced to wait. "I can't do this. Stay here with Ross." She dashed out of the car before Carla had the chance to stop her.

Keeping low, she crossed the country lane and motioned for Will and Barry to remain where they were, then she crouched and followed the hedge line to the entrance of the farmhouse's drive. She watched the team move into action, surround the building. The officer in charge used the megaphone to make contact with Quaker.

Quaker warned them to stay back or he would hurt the hostages. Sara's heart seemed to be in her mouth at this point. She was eager to get in there herself and drag this bastard out, but she held firm, aware of her limits and the bother she would likely get in if she interfered. She had enough problems to deal with, didn't she? Shots sounded. *Shit! Is that Quaker or our guys?*

More shots fired, and the officer in charge again warned Quaker what would happen if he didn't surrender.

Sara's breathing became erratic, fear coursing through her insides for the family involved in this gruelling situation.

Bang, bang! This was followed by men shouting, "Get on the floor, hands above your head."

"You can come out now, Inspector. The suspect has been secured."

Sara emerged from the shadows and approached the commanding officer. "I couldn't resist it. Sorry."

"No harm done, this time. You might want to follow orders in the future, though, for your own safety."

She smiled at him. "I will. Can I go in there?"

"Not yet. We've had to call for an ambulance."

"What? Why? Who got injured?"

"A woman, she seems in a bad way."

"Jesus. I've got her son in the car. I told him nothing would happen to his mum. I know, I shouldn't have said that."

"No, another lesson learnt, eh?"

The man stepped away from her and shouted orders at his team. Sara stood there, in limbo until people spilled out of the house.

Quaker hobbled out, his hands in cuffs. He was secured in the back of the vehicle by one of the armed officers.

She was itching to get inside the house now, if only to comfort Lydia. What had happened to the mother? Where was Elizabeth? She didn't have to wait long to find out.

"Come with me," the commanding officer beckoned her.

She swallowed down the lump blocking her throat and tentatively followed him through the front door. The sound of several people talking and women crying filtered through the shell of the house. She stepped into what appeared to be the kitchen and gasped when she saw Lydia huddled together with her mother. Both appeared to be unharmed. So why the need for the ambulance? Her gaze shifted to the other side of the room. She rushed to stand over the young woman lying on the floor, blood coming from between her legs.

"Elizabeth? Can you hear me?"

Her eyes were half-closed. She moved her head a couple of inches, peered up at Sara and whispered, "I'm sorry. I never meant for any of this to happen."

"It's all right, conserve your strength. Is it the baby?"

"Yes, I think I've lost it." Tears mixed with the snot running from her nose.

Sara nodded. "It's okay, the ambulance is on its way. Hang on."

"I want to die."

"We won't let you die, Elizabeth. Hang in there."

Elizabeth moaned gently, and her eyes closed.

The officer crouching beside her felt her pulse and looked up at Sara. He shook his head...she'd gone.

Emotions took over and guided her next move. She did the sign of the cross over the deceased, something she'd never done in her life before.

She glanced up to see Lydia and Gail staring at her, their eyes wide with shock. She crossed the room. "Are either of you hurt?"

Gail shook her head. "He took it out on her. He wouldn't stop thumping her. No wonder she lost the baby. She sacrificed herself to save us."

"She has to be admired for doing that," Sara replied, peering over her shoulder. "Come on, let's get you out of here."

She helped the mother and daughter to their feet.

"Wait! Ross, did he make it?"

"Yes, he's a brave lad. He's in the car. He hitched a ride with a stranger and came directly to the station."

Relief filled Gail's face. She held out a hand for Sara to take. "I'm sorry for doing what I did."

Sara frowned. "What's that?"

"The complaint. I'll rescind that, I promise."

"If that's what you want, then thank you." She led them out of the house and into the car where the three of them were reunited under Carla's and Sara's watchful, watery gazes.

They drove back to the station. Sara had suggested they should go to hospital to be checked over, but Gail insisted they were okay, although Sara eventually put her foot down and ordered them to get a thorough check over from the resident doctor.

Sara and Carla left the family with the doctor and joined the rest of the team in the incident room. They all congratulated each other on a job well done and then called it a day.

Sara hung around and dropped the family back to their house. Each of them hugged her. As she drove back to her own house, she felt strangely at peace for some reason.

EPILOGUE

Sara was in her office the following day, bright and early. She smiled, reflecting on the scene from the previous night when she'd managed to reunite the Daly family. Now, it was the dreaded end-of-the-month paperwork vying for her attention. She and her intrepid team had accomplished what they'd set out to achieve, bringing the case to a swift conclusion before the last day of February.

At the moment, Micky Quaker was being questioned by Will and Barry. She'd passed the buck on this one, fearing she wouldn't have been able to hold back if she was left in the same room with the bastard. Carla was overseeing the interview in the adjoining room and had been keeping her up to date on their progress. Quaker was furious when Will had let it slip that the baby Elizabeth had been carrying wasn't his. He'd torn up the room, lashing out at the three officers and even attacking his solicitor in the process. They'd managed to restrain him and cuff him to the table so they could conduct the rest of the interview in safety.

After settling down, he confessed that he'd killed the three people because of revenge. He would never have gone down that route had he known the baby wasn't his. Elizabeth had used him. He was distraught when that fact had emerged.

Sara glanced up from her paperwork to see DCI Price standing in her doorway. "Do you have a minute?"

She nodded and gestured for the chief to sit. "What can I do for you, boss?"

"I wanted to have a quick word, make sure you're okay."

"I'm fine." She issued her boss a reassuring smile.

"I'm glad to hear it. You've had a tough ride on this one, Sara. I have good news for you."

She placed her pen down and sat back. "I'm all ears."

"As promised, Mrs Daly has rescinded her complaint and instead sung your praises for rescuing her family."

"Wow, that's excellent news. She needn't have gone the extra mile and done that, not with all she has going on, you know, making funeral arrangements et cetera. Ross is an extremely brave lad. Without him taking us there…well, who knows how all this would have ended?"

"You deserve all the praise, Sara. I never doubted your capabilities, unlike yourself. You need to give yourself a good talking to, my girl, when the shit hits the fan in the future."

"Yes, boss. I had to ring the Atleys last night to tell them about Elizabeth."

"Oh, how did they react?"

"Mixed feelings, I guess. Relieved that the family had been released unharmed but devastated their daughter had died in the process."

"My heart goes out to them. Why do people do it? Have affairs, I mean? I don't think anyone realises the devastation it can cause to those involved. Be it the couple having the affair or, if one of them is married, like Mr Daly, the effect it can have on one's family."

"It's beyond me. I've never had a roving eye, so I really can't contemplate why someone would do it. Mark's more man than I can cope with. I wouldn't have the energy to have two men on the go at the same time. Have you ever done it?"

Carol shook her head. "Nope. Like you, I would never have the energy to keep two men satisfied." She rose from her chair and approached the door. "Talking of which, have you set a date yet?"

Sara giggled. "Umm…I've been a tad busy, boss, solving a case."

"Of course, silly me. Stick me down for an invite, won't you?"

"Your name will be at the top of the list. We're hoping to work out the arrangements over the weekend, providing another urgent case doesn't rear its head in the meantime."

"Good. Let me know. Congratulations again on a job well done. You continue to be the best inspector under me. Keep up the good work."

Sara blushed. "Thank you, boss, I appreciate your kind words."

Until the next case appeared on her desk, she felt good having the chief's backing that she was on the right track with her career. Now all she had to do was sort out her personal life. She could see a busy weekend ahead of her, but it would all be worth it…wouldn't it?

THE END

KEEP IN TOUCH WITH THE AUTHOR

Newsletter
http://smarturl.it/8jtcvv

BookBub
www.bookbub.com/authors/m-a-comley

Blog
http://melcomley.blogspot.com

Join my special Facebook group to take part in monthly giveaways.

Readers' Group

NOTE TO THE READER

Dear Reader,

What a heart-wrenching read that was.

But as usual, Sara and her team came to the rescue in her own inimitable way. A gruesome tale nevertheless, I'm sure you'll agree.

Look out for more Sara Ramsey novels during 2020

In the meantime, perhaps you'll consider reading one of my other thriller series? Have you tried the bestselling, award-winning Justice series yet?

Here's the link to the first book in this gripping, fast-paced thriller series CRUEL JUSTICE

Thank you for your support as always.

M A Comley

Printed in Great Britain
by Amazon

59953082R00104